FLIGHT
OF
EAGLES

The story of the American
Kościuszko Squadron
in the
Polish-Russian War
1919-1920

Robert F. Karolevitz
and
Ross S. Fenn

Published by Brevet Press, Inc.
Copyright © 1974 by Brevet Press, Inc.,
a division of BREVET INTERNATIONAL, INC.
Northwestern Bank Building
Sioux Falls, South Dakota 57102

Library of Congress Catalog Card Number: 74-80769

Hard Cover Edition
ISBN: 88498-022-7

First Printing 1974

Manufactured in The United States Of America

Printed by Modern Press
Sioux Falls, South Dakota

ii

To

Charles R. d'Olive

Marek J. Mazynski

and

Lou Prochut

who directly or indirectly had a part in the
development of this book.

Acknowledgments

As co-authors, we are deeply indebted to many individuals who helped in various ways to make this book a published reality. First of all, Charles R. d'Olive, a World War I ace, made the original suggestion which prompted the basic research for the project. A letter to Lowell Thomas, the world-traveled news commentator, brought a ready response and led Ross Fenn to Brig. Gen. Merian C. Cooper. The latter, in turn, provided the first-hand information about the unique organization which grew out of his intense personal desire to serve the revived Polish State. Marek J. Mazynski, a dedicated son of Poland, sustained the endeavor with his enthusiasm and his generous response to many queries. J. J. Smith, an avid compiler of aviation history, was particularly liberal with his assistance.

It was especially fortunate that—in addition to General Cooper—eight other members of the Kościuszko Squadron themselves were able to contribute directly to the contents of the story. Included in that number were Cedric E. Fauntleroy, Ludomił Rayski, Edward C. Corsi, George M. Crawford, Harmon C. Rorison, Kenneth O. Shrewsbury, John C. Speaks and J. Inglis Maitland. By letter, tape recorder, telephone and in person they provided data and insight without which this chronicle of their Polish odyssey would have lacked the flavor of on-the-scene authenticity.

Cooperating, too, were relatives and friends of the pilots who supplied a wealth of yellowed newspaper clippings, original documents of the historic venture, personal letters of 1919-21 vintage and an invaluable collection of photographs which have added a graphic dimension to the narrative. We are grateful for the cooperation of Mrs. Aleksander Seńkowski, Mrs. Susan Phillips Noble, Mrs. Dorothy H. Cooper, Mrs. Jacquelyn Fauntleroy Green, Mrs. Winifred W. Speaks, Mrs. George M. Crawford, Mrs. K. O. Shrewsbury, Kenneth O. Shrewsbury, Jr., and Mrs. Margaret Devereux Lippit Rorison.

Specific research material came from many sources: John E. Taylor and Kent C. Carter, National Archives and Record Service; Ronald V. Dodds, Canadian Department of National Defence; W. R. Wybraniec, Polish Air Force Association, London; Father Hyacinth Dabrowski, O.F.M., Cap.; John Dec, Polish Army Veterans Association of America; Conrad L. Eckert, Tulsa County Historical Society; John W. Wike, Center of Military History, Department of the Army; Edmund Jungowski, Warsaw, Poland; Bette J. Herrald, El Paso, Texas; Russell Manning, Bronx, New York; Conrey Bryson, El Paso County Historical Society; Natchez, Mississippi, Historical Society; Capt. Roy C. Smith, III, U.S.N.R. (Ret.), U. S. Naval Academy Alumni Association; Mrs. R. Oppman, Keeper of the Archives, The Polish Institute and Sikorski Museum, London; Royal D. Frey and Charles G. Worman, Air Force Museum, Wright-Patterson Air Force Base, Ohio; Wesley H. Poling, Alumni Records Office, Yale University; Frederic J. Gardner, Amherst College Alumni Council; Diane Balboni, Harvard University Alumni Office; Michael M. Phillips, Saratoga National Historical Park; Col. Roy K. Flint, United States Military Academy; Dayton W. Canaday (director) and Bonnie Gardner, South Dakota Historical Resource Center; Robert B. Wood, National Air and Space Museum, Smithsonian Institution; Mrs. Penny Volin, research librarian, Public Library, Sioux Falls, South Dakota; and Les Helgeland, Yankton (S. D.) **Daily Press and Dakotan**.

Acknowledgments

Thanks go also to Jim Deneen for jacket design and the paintings of the Albatros and Balilla airplanes which have added welcome color to the book; to Martha Weatherford for cartographic effects; and to James W. Phillips for research assistance and counsel.

Lastly, we are truly appreciative of the forbearance, patience and understanding shown by our wives—Phyllis and Mary Jane—who, by force of circumstances, were caught up in the project to a point where their lives were disrupted by it. They showed unusual restraint as they listened to war stories **ad infinitum;** and—in many ways—the final product was affected positively by their influence.

To all of the above—and those we may have overlooked inadvertently—we offer a sincere Polish thank-you: "DZIE-KUJE BARDZO!"

—The Authors

Contents

A Guide to Pronunciation

Readers unfamiliar with Polish and Russian pronunciation may have some difficulty with proper nouns and several non-English expressions in this book.

While it is impossible in a paragraph or two to consider all the intricacies of language differences, it is hoped that the brief phonetic guide which follows will enhance reading ease. As in all terse generalizations, however, exceptions and contradictions can occur. In the list of people and places, for instance, a variety of Polish, Russian and common-use English names are included, so—depending upon the spelling—pronunciation will vary accordingly.

Polish-to-English Phonetic Aids

c becomes ts as in bits.

cz is pronounced ch as in choose.

i is generally sounded as ee in feet.

j is usually pronounced as y in yawl.

ł is similar to the English w in yew.

ń is comparable to the n in ing.

ó and u are pronounced as oo in boot.

sz and ś are similar to sh as in shoot.

w is pronounced as v in the middle of a word and as f at the end.

wło becomes vwo and wła is vwah.

Proper Noun Pronunciations

Balilla	Bah-**lee**-la (Italian)
Berdichev	Burr-**dee**-cheff
Belaya Tserkov	Bel-**yea**-ah **Chair**-koff
Budenny	Boo-je-**nay**
Bug (River)	Boog
Cherkasi	**Chair**-ka-see
Chudnov	**Chood**-noff
Fastov	**Faw**-stoff
Kazatin	Kawsh-ah-**teen**
Kiev	Key-**eff**
Kościuszko	Kawsh-**choosh**-ko
Lwów	Lvoof (with the **L** almost blended into the **v**)
Piłsudski	Pee-oo-**soot**-ski
Rozwadowski	Rose-va-**dov**-ski
Słucz (River)	Shwooch
Śmigły-Rydz	Schmick-way **Ridz**
Uman	**Oo**-mahn
Zhitomir	Zhee-**toe**-meer

Foreword

On November 11, 1918, at precisely 11 a.m., Paris time, the Armistice which terminated World War I went into effect.

Headlines throughout the world announced that the war to end all wars was over, but sadly enough there was a contradictory epilogue already in the making—a bloody continuation of the conflict which had ravaged Europe for four frightful years. To most citizens of the United States—overjoyed by the prospects of endless peace and normalcy—it was a virtually unknown, after-the-fact war which would add thousands of victims to the millions already slain in defense of varying philosophies of liberty, national honor and imperialism.

The belligerents were the "new" Poland, a nation officially re-created by the peace-makers at Versailles, and the "new" Bolshevik Russia, a communistic order born out of a revolution of the proletariat. The historical events, the political intrigue and the ideological concepts involved in the conflict of Slavic peoples were complex and confusing. Polish-Russian antagonisms were centuries old, being periodically enflamed by petty border disputes, shifts of power and occasional major military confrontations; and when Poland was returned to the map of Europe after an absence of almost a century and a quarter, the fears and mutual distrust were likewise revived.

However, to a small coterie of American flying officers who offered their services to the Polish cause, the age-old animosities and political entanglements of the past were of little consequence. What they really understood was that a newly restored Poland (and possibly the rest of Europe) was being threatened by a massive, revolution-spawned Red Army before the final peace treaties of World War I were even signed. Adventuresome and idealistic, the young airmen—a majority of whom were veterans of the American Expeditionary Force—volunteered generously to extend their European crusade for the defense of another nation's freedom, and this heroic story is the result of their commitment.

As members of the unique Kościuszko Squadron, they fought under the White Eagle of Poland, not as mercenary hirelings but as dedicated compatriots. Not one of them was of Polish ancestry. Most of the military action in which they participated occurred in Galicia and the Ukraine where techniques of ancient and modern warfare met head-on as pilots of patched-up aircraft attacked Cossack cavalrymen not far removed from their medieval predecessors.

This epic tale has been pieced together from the diaries, letters and personal reminiscences of the intrepid Americans who wore the distinctive uniforms of the embryonic Polish Air Service. Especially contributing to the authenticity of the story were the private papers of Brig. Gen. Merian C. Cooper (1893-1973), who conceived the basic idea of a volunteer unit; the correspondence and collected effects of Col. Cedric E. Fauntleroy (1891-1963), the squadron's first commander; the detailed long-hand memoirs of Capt. Edward C. Corsi (1898-1971); and the recollections of Maj. George M. (Buck) Crawford, who arrived with the original contingent and who later succeeded Cooper as the group's third commanding officer. Co-author Ross S. Fenn devoted more than a decade to the accumulation of these fascinating mementoes of a little known war, and it was largely from his diligent research that this saga has been reconstructed.

The logbooks of the squadron itself were an invaluable source of information and provided the continuing thread for the story. Unfortunately (from an author's point of view), the flyers had more to do than record the events of the day, and often—when action was most intense—just a single sentence or two unemotionally capsuled the bravest deeds or the greatest drama. Also, because none of the Americans had a complete command of the Polish or Russian languages, their spelling of place names and other local references was often unique and inconsistent. Sometimes as many as three versions of a single town appeared in the same report.

This point is mentioned because an effort was made by the authors to standardize names for the reader's benefit; otherwise, when excerpts or direct quotations were taken from the log or other memorabilia, only minor editing for clarity was involved. A final, rather arbitary choice of place-name spellings was developed from **Webster's Geographical Dictionary** and the maps of The National Geographic Society. Much of the confusion was caused, incidentally, because many cities and towns in the area in which the Kościuszko Squadron operated had two or more names, usually including a Polish and a Russian version. The authors adopted the latter in the eastern sector (generally beyond the Słucz River) and the former in the western or Galician zone.

Such details, of course, in no way affected the activities of the men involved. What they did is the important element of the story, and in that regard a concerted effort was made to place this account into proper perspective against the backdrop of history rather than to present their exploits as an isolated aviation experience. The heroics, the drama, the suspense and the action which characterized the squadron's role in "the forgotten war" of 1919-20 give the episode an almost fiction-like self-sufficiency—but viewed in the light of Poland's past and the subsequent events which occurred in Europe during the ensuing two decades, the military contributions of the young Americans who flew in behalf of a beleagured, restored nation take on a much greater significance.

The prologue which follows skips fleetingly across ten centuries of Polish heritage, an abbreviation which the authors recognize can lead to generalization and over-simplification. (Not even included, for instance, is a description of the centuries-old Polish-Lithuanian union which would justify more than a volume of its own.) Hopefully, though, this necessary condensation is inclusive enough to set the stage so that the adventures of the Yankee airmen can be accorded the historical importance they truly deserve.

Robert F. Karolevitz
Ross S. Fenn

From Kosynierzy Warszawscy by Kazimerz Wegrzecki, courtesy of Veritas Foundation Publication Center, London, England.

Tadeusz Kościuszko (1746-1817), Polish patriot and hero of the American Revolution, was an appropriate namesake for the squadron of military airmen from the United States who volunteered to fight for the preservation of Poland's newly restored freedom following World War I.

Prologue

Poland Shall Never Die--While We Yet Live

Tadeusz Andrzej Bonawentura Kościuszko never saw an airplane. The Polish patriot died in Switzerland on October 15, 1817, having participated with his sword in the birthing of the United States of America and, ironically enough, in the total obliteration from the map of Europe of his beloved Poland.

It was appropriately fitting, therefore, that more than a century later his name should be adopted by a squadron of American military pilots who volunteered in 1919 to fight for the preservation of the Polish nation just as the 30-year-old Kościuszko had offered his services to the Continental Congress in August of 1776.

To put the ensuing narrative into historical focus, it is necessary to review in capsule form the Polish tradition and the circumstances which—over a period of many, many years—led ultimately to the creation of the Kościuszko Squadron. It is a complicated story of triumph and turmoil, moments of peace and interludes of insurrection, great pomp and power, and then, finally, national oblivion (except in the hearts of the people who survived).

The recorded history of Poland, as a geographic and governmental entity, had its beginning in the middle of the 10th Century when the whole of continental Europe was suffering labor pains of the multiple birth of nations. At that time a Western Slavic tribe known as the Polanie had risen to a position of strength around the fortified town of Gniezno, almost on a line half way between the modern cities of Berlin and Warsaw. Leadership of the Polanie had passed into the hands of Mieszko I, who, according to tradition, had been born sightless and then miraculously cured of his blindness at the age of seven.

As he led his warriors to dominance over adjacent tribes, Mieszko became increasingly aware of other civilizations beyond his pagan domain, and—whether accidentally or by design—he gradually established contact with his Christianized Germanic and Slavic neighbors. This liaison resulted ultimately in Mieszko's marriage in 965 to Princess Dabrowka, daughter of Boleslav I of Bohemia. As was the custom of his people, the Polanie chieftain already had seven wives when he met Dabrowka, and she, being a devout Catholic and niece of St. Wenceslaus, presumably refused Mieszko's hand until he had dissolved his polygamous union.

In the following year (966), the Polish leader—through his wife's intercession—accepted the teachings of Christianity and was baptized. This milestone event marked the emergence of Poland as a Catholic state, as Mieszko placed his people and his land beneath the papal banner, an act which in turn opened the region to the cultural, religious and political influences of the more developed nations. Throughout the ensuing centuries the Catholic heritage dating back to Mieszko's conversion was to be a dominant factor in the Polish national epic, manifesting itself in missionary zeal during periods of power and serving as an unbreakable thread of faith and hope when Poland languished under alien rule.

From its beginning, Poland was, in the words of historian H. G. Wells, "surrounded by enemies instead of by the sea." War became an integral part of her development, with her borders expanding and contracting as a result of each new conflict. For purposes of this prologue, however, there is no need to chronicle the seemingly endless battles or the political

complexities brought on by a long succession of rulers, not all of whom were motivated by a burning desire to build a strong, benevolently governed, independent state. For almost two centuries—from 1138 to 1314—Poland was divided internally into self-centered principalities with very little national cohesion. The return to a more centralized government and the emergence of a Renaissance spirit was disrupted by the Reformation movement which, surprisingly enough, gave early evidence of catching on in a predominantly Catholic setting. In final result, though, only limited numbers of the aristocratic elite were won over to the various forms of Protestantism which failed to take root among the peasantry. The net effect, as it turned out, was to provide the Poles with a rallying point around their traditional religion.

Having survived the theological crisis, Poland subjected herself to new problems of her own making: political reforms which were theoretically promising but seriously deficient in practice. The first was the conversion of the governmental form from a limited monarchy to a republic with an elective king. Unfortunately, the latter was to have no choice of successor. He was to marry a wife selected for him by the senate, one of two houses of the parliamentary body (the **Sejm**). He was to be neutral in all religious matters; he could make neither peace nor war, levy a tax nor alter the law.

The regal elections which followed were dominated by foreign money and foreign pressures; and because of petty jealousies among the Polish gentry, the selection of alien kings became the general practice. Added to that, the principle of the "free veto" was written into the constitution, permitting any deputy in the **Sejm** to kill a legislative act merely by arising and declaring "I disapprove." Later, use of the "free veto" was broadened so that a single vote could dissolve a parliamentary session and negate all its actions. Needless to say, this concept, which was based on the lofty principle of individual equality for all **Sejm** members, made state business difficult if not impossible to perform. One bribe could obstruct a minor

law or destroy the work of an entire legislative session. An ineffectual king added to the government's inability to function. As H. G. Wells wrote: "Poland was not simply a crowned aristocratic republic like the British, it was a **paralyzed** crowned aristocratic republic."

Somehow, though, the nation managed to exist for another two centuries, winning and losing wars, being plundered systematically by Swedes, Saxons, and Russians, and, in general, growing weaker with each passing decade under the debilitating effects of the feudal anarchy. The stage was set, either for internal revolt and revival, or for even greater national humiliation.

Sadly enough, the second alternative prevailed. In the latter half of the 18th Century, the reigning powers of Europe included Catherine the Great of Russia, Frederick the Great of Prussia and Maria Theresa, the Austrian queen. Each of them had designs on portions of their emaciated neighbor, and in 1772 this unlikely triumvirate conspired to accomplish the First Partition of Poland by which they divided 80,686 square miles of territory and more than 1,700,000 inhabitants. At the same time a new constitution—which continued the destructive principles of an elective monarch and the "free veto"—was installed, making what remained of the Polish state dependent upon its despoilers.

While all this was transpiring, a young military student named Tadeusz Kościuszko was completing his training in France where he was especially schooled in fortification techniques, engineering and artillery. When he returned to Poland in 1774, the 28-year-old captain could not possibly have imagined the strange progression of circumstances which would ultimately immortalize him in the histories of two nations. Born in the village of Mereczowszczyzna near Brest-Litovsk on February 12, 1746, he was the youngest of four children in a family of modest means with patents of nobility. Following a preparatory education typical of his social class, young Tadeusz, at 19, was admitted to the Corps of Cadets of the

Royal Military School in Warsaw where he studied for three years. Because of his scholarship, he attracted the personal attention of Stanisław Augustus II Paniatowski, the last king of Poland, and it was through the latter's beneficence that Kościuszko was sent to France to complete his formal training.

The First Partition was already a completed reality when the talented captain came home, but—like most officers his age—he apparently was more swept up in the social affairs of the waning aristocracy than in patriotically inspired plans for revolution. Unfortunately, the residue from the family estate (his father died when he was 12) could not support him adequately, and so he found employment as a tutor for the daughters of a provincial hetman. He promptly fell in love with one of the ladies, and—according to a popular version of the affair—as the young couple made preparations for an elopement, he was wounded by her father's retainers and driven from the estate.

The year was 1776, and possibly motivated more by the miseries of his romantic failures than by fervor for a far-away revolution, Captain Kościuszko left Poland, partly on borrowed money, to seek fame and fortune in the newly formed army of the United States. Commissioned as a colonel of engineers, Kościuszko was assigned to the staff of Gen. Horatio Gates, who recognized the newcomer's talents and utilized them at Saratoga, Ticonderoga, West Point, Bemis Heights and Stillwater on the Hudson. Later Gates wrote: ". . . . the great tacticians of the campaign were hills and forests which a young Polish Engineer was skillful enough to select . . . ." Afterwards, Colonel Kościuszko also distinguished himself in the southern sector under Gen. Nathaniel Greene where he had the unique experience of leading an attack against a British foraging party on James Island, South Carolina, on November 15, 1782, in what has been considered to be the final military action of the war. In 1783 Kościuszko was rewarded for his devotion to the cause of

American independence with the official thanks of Congress, an almost paltry monetary settlement and a brevet commission of brigadier general. On July 15, 1784, he sailed for Europe after almost eight full years in America, to which he later referred as "my second country."

Meanwhile, as Colonel Kościuszko had fought to secure the freedom of a new nation, his own native Poland was struggling to stay alive under the conditions of the First Partition. After the initial shock, the Poles launched a somewhat belated effort to revitalize their shrunken state. On May 3, 1791, the **Sejm** adopted a new constitution which established a hereditary, limited monarchy, did away with the "free veto," granted absolute religious tolerance, reduced the power of the landed gentry and brought the peasants under the protection of the law. Unfortunately, Russia considered the new constitution "tyrannous and revolutionary," and, as a direct consequence, another war was declared.

By this time Tadeusz Kościuszko had returned to Poland and was installed as one of the commanders of the tiny Polish army of less than 50,000 men. For more than three months the small force held off the invader, winning three key battles and then falling back strategically to defend the capital. At that point King Stanisław—a former lover of Catherine the Great—apparently lost his nerve and, under pressure from internal conspirators, ordered an end to the resistance. Kościuszko and other patriots like him fled the country in indignation rather than defeat. The constitution of May 3 was abolished, and ultimately the Second Partition of 1793 became a direct result of the abbreviated conflict. This time Poland was reduced to less than one-third her original size and left with a population of just three and a half million people.

Meanwhile, General Kościuszko and other Polish nationalists assembled in Leipzig were they made plans for a liberation movement. Their resources were extremely limited, their support (beyond their own numbers) was virtually nonexistent, and, to their further disadvantage, a passionate enthusiasm for the cause tended to blind them to practical realities. Despite the odds, however, in March of 1794 Kościuszko went to Kraków where he assumed the powers of a benevolent dictator and declared a national insurrection. The constitution of May 3 was reaffirmed, with the additional proviso that serfdom was at an end and that all peasants would henceforth be free.

The rural poor in particular responded to Kościuszko's call to service, and his rag-tag army (reminiscent of the revolutionary forces he had known in America) launched a new attack on the Russians. Again initial successes were achieved; Warsaw was recaptured; and almost three-quarters of the ancient territory was recovered. To Kościuszko's chagrin, however, the total involvement of the entire Polish citizenry was eroded by mob lawlessness of his own people in the cities and the selfish unwillingness of most of the aristocracy to support his cause. Concurrently, the hostility of Prussia and Austria—the other two partitioning powers—was aroused, and gradually the opposing forces were increased to a level of overwhelming superiority. After a brilliant defense of Warsaw, on October 10, 1794, Kościuszko personally led a Polish army of 7,000 men in an attack on a Russian force of more than twice that number at Maciejowice. When the relief support on which he had counted failed to arrive, Kościuszko and his troops were routed and the general himself was seriously wounded and captured. Again Warsaw fell, and by the terms of the treaties which followed in 1795 and 1796, Russia, Prussia and Austria effected the Third Partition which completely wiped the name Poland from the map of Europe.

In the aftermath, General Kościuszko recovered and was released. Beginning in 1797 he spent more than a year in the United States where he was warmly welcomed and entertained by his former comrades in arms. Many of his officers and men, meanwhile, had emigrated to Italy where they formed a Polish legion which fought for Napoleon in Europe,

Africa and the West Indies. Kościuszko, who returned to France in the wake of the revolution there, was presumably offered a position of high command by the First Consul, but the Polish patriot refused unless the liberation of his country received high priority in Napoleon's plans. Such a promise was not forthcoming, and the aging general went into retirement at the country estate of a friend at Berville, near Paris. Later, while sojourning in Switzerland, he died at the age of 71. He was buried on Wawel Hill at Kraków where earlier he had taken an oath of fidelity to the Polish nation. He was, as Thomas Jefferson wrote, "as pure a son of liberty as I have ever known."

For the 123 years which followed, Poland existed only in the spirit of the people, bolstered by the Roman Catholic faith which was the principle factor distinguishing the Polish population from Orthodox Russians and Protestant Prussians. Abortive uprisings in 1830 and 1863 were beaten down and Kościuszko's dream of a reborn Poland seemed surely to have been interred with him and the other patriots who perished in unsuccessful insurrection attempts after his death.

Earlier Stanisław Staszyc, Polish political and social reformer, had written: "A great nation can fall, but only an unworthy nation can perish." Following the Third Partition, Poles everywhere seemingly clutched to that basic philosophy and—consciously or subconsciously—assumed that one day their cherished land would be freed again to pursue her God-given mission, about which poet Zygmunt Krasinski had theorized in his nationalistic **Psalm of Faith** in 1845.

It is understandable, then, that World War I, which wreaked historic revenge on the partitioning conspirators, was greeted by Polish patriots as the eagerly awaited, miraculous response to millions of fervent prayers. On November 5, 1916—while the military situation was still favorable to them—the Central Powers announced the establishment of a limited "Polish Kingdom," a puppet government headed by a Regency Council appointed by the Austrian and German emperors. The fortunes of war reversed themselves in 1918, and when Austria-Hungary capitulated on November 3, the Polish government in Warsaw proclaimed a "People's Poland." In the meantime, President Woodrow Wilson revealed his famous Fourteen Points, the thirteenth of which stated:

> An independent Polish state should be erected which would include the territories inhabited by indisputably Polish populations, which should be assured a free and secure access to the sea, and whose political and economic independence and territorial integrity should be guaranteed by international convenant.

Three days after the signing of the Armistice, the Regency Council resigned and all its powers were transferred to Józef Piłsudski, former Socialist revolutionary, who—like Tadeusz Kościuszko—was a product of the Lithuanian portion of the old joint commonwealth. Almost eight months later—on June 28, 1919—Roman Dmowski and Ignacy Jan Paderewski signed the Treaty of Versailles on behalf of the restored Republic of Poland, an action which, in effect, legitimized what had already occurred. More than a century after his death, Kościuszko's dreams had been fulfilled, and the words of the Polish national anthem—written in 1797 by Józef Wybicki, Kościuszko's adjutant—rang out more clearly than ever: "Poland shall not perish while her sons yet live!"

1746

IN MEMORY OF

1817

THE NOBLE SON OF POLAND

BRIG. GENERAL

THADDEUS KOSCIUSZKO

MILITARY ENGINEER

SOLDIER OF THE WAR OF INDEPENDENCE

WHO, UNDER COMMAND OF GENERAL GATES

SELECTED AND FORTIFIED THESE FIELDS

FOR THE GREAT BATTLE OF SARATOGA

IN WHICH THE INVADER WAS VANQUISHED

AND AMERICAN FREEDOM ASSURED

ERECTED BY HIS COMPATRIOTS

A. D. 1936

KOSCIUSZKO

The services of Tadeusz Kościuszko to the American Colonies during the Revolutionary War are commemorated by this monument at the Saratoga National Historical Park in New York State. The Polish officer remained in the United States for almost eight years.

Chapter I

For Kościuszko and Pulaski: A Favor Returned

At seven a.m. on February 14, 1919, in the town of Bereza Kartuska, approximately 140 miles south of Wilno, five Polish officers with 57 men engaged a small unit of Bolsheviks occupying the remote Lithuanian site. In the course of the skirmish, 80 Red Army soldiers were taken prisoner—but of far greater historical consequence, the Polish-Soviet War of 1919-20 had begun, without official declaration or detailed strategy on the part of either foe.

For generations to come, students of European history will be attempting to unravel all the factors, philosophies, traditional animosities and precipitous events which brought about still another major armed conflict at a most illogical time (if, of course, there is ever a logical time for war). Neither of the adversaries was prepared for additional bloodletting, for further depletion of resources or for the new demands on a physically and emotionally drained citizenry. But war came nonetheless, and the complexities of the issues involved were little known to the actual combatants who fought either because they had to or because they truly believed in their respective basic causes: the extension of the Bolshevik ideology to the whole of Europe on one hand, and the preservation and expansion of the recreated Poland on the other.

In brief, the politico-military realities were these:

Between Poland and Russia the border areas—from Latvia and Lithuania southward through Byelorussia and the Ukraine—had vital meaning to both sides. To Polish leaders, the borderlands had to be preserved one way or another as a bulwark against the traditional enemy to the east, either as independent entities receptive to the needs of Poland's national security or under direct influence or control from Warsaw. To the Bolsheviks, the border regions constituted the great land bridge westward over which the Communist revolution would be carried all the way to the Atlantic.

Late in 1918 in the northern sector, the **Oberkommando-Ostfront** or Eastern defense line of the capitulated Central Powers was still manned by an unbeaten, disciplined German army which the allies permitted to remain in position after the Armistice as a stabilizing force between Poland and Russia until the machinery of peace began functioning properly. There were other factors involved, of course, but in simplistic terms, when General Max Hoffman's German army was finally evacuated from the **Ober-Ost** beginning in December, 1918, a vacuum was created into which both Polish and Soviet forces were drawn. Military confrontation was inevitable (whether or not, as historians continue to argue, it was desired by either side at that particular time), and the isolated clash at Bereza Kartuska was the insignificant beginning of a most significant but seriously misunderstood war.

In the meantime, as the direct conflict between Poland and the Bolsheviki had its inauspicious inception in the northern sector, another series of events was unfolding south of the Pripet Marshes. In the Galician district (once known as **Malopolska** or Little Poland), the incursion of Ukrainian nationalists had extended itself westward to the ancient city of Lwów, site of one of Eastern Europe's oldest universities and for centuries a prominent center of Polish culture. The Ukraine, like Poland, was experiencing the hyperdynamia of sudden independence and was literally a cauldron of military and political confusion which seethed internally and bubbled over at the borders. Part of that foment manifested itself in an intense desire to include Eastern Galicia within the bounds of the new state, and during the night of October 31, 1918, Ukrainian conspirators, supported by Austrian regiments composed largely of their own compatriots, occupied all government buildings and points of strategic importance in Lwów.

With the dawn, the sight of the blue and yellow flag of the Ukraine flying over the city hall struck the predominant Polish population first with a momentary sense of bewilderment and then with an explosion of passionate anger. The ultimate conclusion was an especially proud moment in Polish history. Lwów—then called Lemberg as the result of Austria's earlier role in the partitioning duplicity—had been virtually stripped of able-bodied Poles of military age. Moreover, it was reported that only 64 rifles were available to the young boys, old men, disabled veterans and gallant women of all ages who assumed the unquestioned task of driving the Ukrainians from their city.

Polish heritage boasts proudly of the heroics of the citizens of Lwów—intense patriots who prayed fervently, battled fiercely and died bravely in the house-to-house, street-by-street fighting which followed. The city was eventually retaken, but at various locations throughout Eastern Galicia, Podolia and Volhynia, clashes between Poles and Ukrainians occurred during the remainder of 1918 and into the new year. It was the type of borderland conflict which Winston Churchill belittingly described to David Lloyd George on the night of the Armistice: "The war of the giants has ended; the quarrels of the pygmies have begun."

With the end of World War I hostilities, the gargantuan task of undoing the damages of man's inhumanity to man received the immediate attention of the victorious Allied powers. As one of the major agencies devoted to the abatement of human suffering, Herbert Hoover's American Relief Adminis-

tration quickly extended its mission of mercy into Poland and
other long-buffeted areas of central Europe; and from Warsaw a young American Air Service officer, Captain Merian
Coldwell Cooper, was dispatched to the Galician district to
attempt delivery of desperately needed rations into embattled
Lwów. Writing at a later date, Cooper described the circumstances of his assignment:

> I took a train immediately to Przemyśl. I
> rounded up loads of flour and other food sup-
> plies . . . The rail line and the road were both
> cut by the Ukrainians. But I went forward and
> fought with a battalion of Poznań Poles. We
> opened up both the rail line and road after a
> couple of days of severe combat, and I carried my
> flour and food stuff through . . . I found Lwów
> was indeed a town starving, the Polish inhabi-
> tants' spirit unbroken.

Now, to bring all of these events into perspective for purposes of this particular story, it must be remembered that
the Polish-Ukrainian involvement in the beginning was **not**
a directly related part of Poland's war against the Bolsheviks.
Later, however, the Ukraine was to figure heavily in the
greater conflict, the first scattered engagements of which
were already taking place in the north as Captain Cooper
continued delivering food, clothing and medical supplies to
the indomitable Lwówians. Meanwhile, in the course of his
work he watched the resolute Poles battle the usurpers with
whatever weapons they could get their hands on; and over
and over again he heard about the fearless actions of women
and young girls, of the incomparable Schoolboy Legion, of
cripples and old men who courageously overturned the
Ukrainian coup. The unrelenting tenacity of these ill-
equipped, under-fed and loosely organized patriots was in-
delibly impressed upon the American captain's mind, and it
became increasingly obvious to him that he personally would
have to do more than relief work in behalf of the Polish cause.

In the colonial days Merian Cooper's Scottish-English forebearers had settled on the banks of the St. Marys River which later became part of the boundary between the states of Georgia and Florida. The captain himself had been born in Jacksonville, Florida, on October 24, 1894, and as a youngster he had often been told the story of his great, great grandfather—Colonel John Cooper—who in 1779 had assisted the mortally wounded Casimir Pulaski from the Revolutionary War battlefield at Savannah, Georgia, and had him carried to a ship in the harbor where the Polish officer died. Count Pulaski, like Tadeusz Kościuszko, had volunteered to fight for the American cause against the British, and during the course of his service in the southern colonies, he became a personal friend of John Cooper, a cavalry commander whom he [Pulaski] trained in the art of swordsmanship. It is conceivable, too, that Colonel Cooper also knew Kościuszko, since the latter had likewise seen action in the southland during the closing stages of the war.

With that family tradition as inspiration, it is understandable why the 26-year-old captain was frustrated in his role as a dispenser of relief goods. His experiences at Lwów convinced him that Poland was also in desperate need of military assistance. More than that, he had begun to develop a strong aversion to Marxist communism, an antipathy which was to stay with him and grow in intensity throughout his lifetime. When relief supplies began to reach the City of the Lion with sufficient regularity to overcome the crisis condition, Captain Cooper returned to Warsaw to seek greater involvement. On May 19, 1919, he wrote a letter through channels to the commanding general of the A.E.F. at Chaumont, France, which read in part:

> I request to be assigned to duty either in the Air Service or the Infantry in Archangel where our troops are in action against the enemy. . . . . The American Food Administration is willing to

release me immediately if I may be assigned to
such service. . . . .If [it is] impossible to station
me with our own troops, I request to be assigned
to duty with any of the Allied units in Archangel
or with the Russian or Polish Armies fighting
against the Bolsheviks.

The letter was endorsed by William R. Grove, head of the
Food Administration's mission to Poland, and forwarded to
Herbert Hoover's offices in Paris. Cooper was cited for having "handled a very difficult situation in the City of Lemberg
during the seige," and his request for transfer was approved,
pending A.E.F. concurrence. Meanwhile, he apparently
sought quicker action and pursued another course which he
himself described:

I got General [Tadeusz] Rozwadowski to take
me to the Chief-of-State, Marshal Piłsudski. I
immediately offered to resign from the United
States Armed Forces to join the Polish Air
Force. The Marshal misunderstood one thing.
He thought I wished to become a soldier of fortune for money. I jumped to my feet and told
him I would accept no promotion in rank until
I earned it in battle, and that I would never accept one cent over and above what a Polish officer received. The fiery, piercing eyes of the
Marshal looked at me for a second; then he stood
and clasped my hand.

With a commitment from Marshal Piłsudski to bolster
him, Captain Cooper was ordered back to Paris for demobilization from the U. S. Air Service. At that time—in the
early summer of 1919—his plan of action was relatively un-
charted, but he was resolutely certain of one thing: his fierce
desire to confront Bolshevism on the field of battle.

As the train from Warsaw traveled westward across Germany toward the French capital, Captain Cooper had plenty of time for reflection. He had already survived one war, and his hands and face still bore the scars of the flaming crash on September 26, 1918, when his plane was shot down behind the German lines. The American Expeditionary Force headquarters later issued a memorial certificate of his death, but Cooper was very much alive when he assisted his wounded observer—1st Lt. Edmund C. Leonard—from the burning D.H. 4. Both men had been promptly captured, and Cooper spent the remaining weeks of the war recovering from his injuries in a German prison hospital near Breslau.

For the flight resulting in his capture, Captain Cooper was recommended for the Distinguished Service Cross, but after the Armistice, when he was recuperating further in the Red Cross hospital at Neuilly, France, he wrote a letter to the chief of the Decorations Section of the A.E.F. in which he said:

> I respectfully request that the recommendation made that I receive the Distinguished Service Cross be disapproved . . . .When I first understood that I had been recommended, I was very pleased as I appreciate the high honor, but after long thought and consideration I realize it would be unjust and unfair for me to receive any honor consideration which the six other officers who fell in flames in the same flight, and so died, did not receive. There was absolutely nothing more courageous in my conduct than in that of the dead and living of my comrades. . . .I do not wish this to effect [sic] in any manner the recommendation for my observer, Lt. Edmund Leonard, whose worthiness was far greater than my own.

Corsi Collection

That action was typical of the young, impetuous Air Service officer who earlier had resigned from the United States Naval Academy in 1915, the year he should have been graduated. His advocacy of military air power—than an unpopular concept among most aging Navy officers—was involved in his decision; but, as he himself was quick to admit, he also was short in navigation course grades and long on disciplinary demerits. (In later years he described his departure from Annapolis quite simply: "There was nothing dishonorable connected with my resignation. I was high-spirited, loved excitement, took chances and got caught too many times.") One of his nicknames at the Naval Academy was "Alligator Joe," and the school's yearbook of 1915 had this to say about him:

> His heart is as large as his possibilities and
> . . . . Wherever he goes, his "sovereign state of
> Florida" will ever feel the honor and distinction
> of claiming such a son as he. Cooper, we like you
> because you are a man of original ideas; a man
> of practical experience; a man of strong convic-
> tion, and a man of remarkable personality.

With his short-lived Navy career ended, Cooper enlisted in the Second Georgia Infantry of the National Guard and served on the Mexican border during the campaign against Pancho Villa. Thereafter he twice turned down commissions in favor of aviation training as a private first class. On September 26, 1917—exactly one year to the day prior to his

———

(opposite page)

Capt. Merian C. Cooper—impetuous, imaginative and idealistic—conceived the idea of a volunteer force to help the Poles fight the Bolsheviks. He was tough enough to survive both German and Russian prisons; he lived to serve again in World War II, ultimately attaining the rank of brigadier general.

ill-fated flight over Germany—he received his wings as a Reserve Military Aviator at Mineola Field, Long Island, New York.

It was not the least bit unusual, then, that Captain Cooper—the "man of strong conviction"—had committed himself to another war, one in which he seemingly had neither a direct national nor personal interest, and as his train pulled into the Paris station, he could hardly have predicted the fateful unfolding of events which followed during the next several weeks.

———

The unexpected but opportune reunion of Captain Cooper and Major Cedric E. Fauntleroy at a little sidewalk cafe near the Place de L'Alma in Paris was to have a far-reaching effect, not only upon each of them as individuals but upon the new Polish Republic which by July of 1919 was spasmodically at war with Bolshevik Russia from the Rumanian border northward through Byelorussia. For a variety of reasons, though, there was a general lull in direct military action following the capture of Wilno by the Poles in late April. The hiatus was understandable. The Soviets had multiple distractions internally, not to mention a major threat from Anton Ivanovich Denikin's White Army advancing toward Moscow from the south. Polish officials, meanwhile, were busy trying to organize and equip an effective military force from a hodgepodge of units and individuals struggling home from various World War I fronts in every imaginable kind of uniform.

The two American Air Service officers, who renewed acquaintances in the pleasant surrounding of the outdoor cafe, had known one another briefly at the A.E.F.'s first aviation training center at Issoudon, France, after which their orders had sent them to different combat units: Fauntleroy to the famed 94th Hat-in-the-Ring Squadron and Cooper to the 20th Squadron of the First Day Bombardment Group. The major had heard of Cooper's apparently fatal crash in Germany and not of his capture and ultimate release, so he was momentarily taken aback when he first saw his fellow airman alive and well. But following that dramatic instant, the two men exchanged highlights of their personal adventures, and then suddenly the subject of Poland's war against the Bolsheviks manifested itself as a topic of mutual interest.

Fauntleroy—whose war-time experience had been devoted primarily to procuring, assembling and testing planes for A.E.F. flyers—announced that he had signed a contract to go to Warsaw as a paid technical adviser. Cooper, in turn, revealed his somewhat sketchy plan for organizing a volunteer unit to aid the Polish cause. The major agreed that the thought was intriguing, and immediately they turned their attention to the mechanics of converting the idea into reality. The more they talked, the more the concept excited and challenged them. What finally emerged from their animated conversation that sunny, summer afternoon in Paris was the genesis of the Kościuszko Squadron—a coterie of American pilots who would repay a long-standing Revolutionary War debt to Poland. The next step, of course, was to find the men who believed as they did.

———

General Tadeusz Rozwadowski, whom Cooper had known at Lwów, was then chief of the Polish Military Mission at the French capital. His support of the plan for an American volunteer aviation unit was demonstrably enthusiastic, and the facilities of his office were made available for the necessary recruiting campaign. Moreover, he signed a letter of authority which gave official status to the endeavor.

Major C. E. Fauntleroy and Captain M. C. Cooper are hereby enlisted as pilots in the Polish Aviation service with the rank of major and captain respectively and are also authorized to enlist, in addition to themselves, seven other pilots, one with the rank of captain, and six with the

rank of first lieutenant, and two observers, one
with the rank of captain and one with the rank
of first lieutenant. These officers will agree to
serve in the Polish army under the command
of the proper Polish military authorities under
exactly the same conditions as Polish officers of
the same rank for such a period of time as may
be agreed upon enlistment, this time not to ex-
ceed one year. The Polish military authorities
agree to transport these officers from Paris to
Warsaw. This document is not to be considered
in any way as affecting the contract of Major
Fauntleroy with the Roma mission.

Although the majority of experienced A.E.F. pilots had
already returned to the United States following the Armistice,
Cooper and Fauntleroy were mutually determined to be as
selective as possible in their choice of flying comrades. Both
men knew of the woeful lack of equipment which faced them
on the Polish-Soviet front, not to mention the marginal living
conditions, minimal pay, language differences and totally unpredictable combat assignments. Survival and success would
demand skill, resourcefulness, physical and mental toughness,
a spirit of elan and adventure, innate courage, and, for good
measure, dedication to the cause of Poland. Finding people to
fit such stiff qualifications would not be easy, but Cooper and
Fauntleroy, having made their own personal commitments,
began at once to search for appropriate volunteers.

Together they visited the favored Parisian haunts of
American officers. By phone and cablegram they traced down
potential candidates. The quest continued through the remainder of July and into the following month. Finally, on
August 26, the major and the captain reported to General
Rozwadowski that, counting themselves, they had eight stal-
wart airmen ready to fight for Poland just as soon as they
could be officially signed up, equipped and transported to
the war zone.

First came Lt. George Marter Crawford, who had returned to Paris from his assignment with the American Relief Administration in the Baltic region. A trim six-footer, "Buck" Crawford was born in Bristol, Pennsylvania, and had been a Lehigh University fullback before his enlistment in the Air Service in May of 1917. After preliminary ground training at Massachusetts Institute of Technology, he was sent to Mineola Field, Long Island, for flight instruction, and, upon earning his wings, he was among the first U.S. aviators ordered to France. Like Cooper and Fauntleroy, he was assigned to the training center at Issoudon prior to his transfer to a combat squadron. On September 12, 1918—on an observation flight in support of the St. Mihiel drive—his plane was forced down in German territory, and Crawford was taken prisoner (exactly two weeks before Cooper was captured).

Volunteering at the same time was Lt. Kenneth O. Shrewsbury, a native of Charleston, West Virginia. The dapper, mustached graduate of Amherst College had been a law student at Harvard University before he enlisted as a private in the Aviation Section of the U. S. Signal Corps. His stops along the way also included M.I.T., Mineola Field and Issoudon. His law training got him sidetracked from flying for much of his A.E.F. service as he was assigned as an Air Service supply officer at Tours, France. Prior to the Armistice, however, he escaped his desk job and returned to the cockpit, ferrying planes from England to the continent. Before being invited to enlist in the Polish adventure, Shrewsbury and Crawford were about to embark on an automobile tour of Europe, financed largely by the latter's backlog of pay which had accrued during his German imprisonment.

From Brooklyn, New York, Edward C. Corsi joined the select group following service with the occupation forces at Germersheim, Germany. In 1916—at the age of 18—he had gone to Europe as a volunteer ambulance driver; later he signed on with the French Foreign Legion from which he transferred to the French Aviation Service where he was trained as a pilot in the Bleriot School at Avord. As a member of Escadrille Spad 77, he had been wounded twice by pursuing Fokkers following his unassisted destruction of a German observation balloon. Before he lost consciousness, he brought his plane down behind Allied lines and consequently escaped capture. He was taken to a French hospital where he recovered without complications, but his bullet-riddled Spad was so badly damaged that it could not be repaired.

Captain Corsi brought an additional member to the growing organization, a mild-mannered native of Kansas, Carl H. Clark. The latter officer had also worn the uniform of France during World War I, and at 30 was the oldest of the volunteers. He had met Corsi in Paris and was promptly introduced to Cooper and Fauntleroy. Clark's apparently limited aviation experience was understandably questioned, but his obvious desire to participate proved to be an overbalancing factor in his favor.

The seventh volunteer, Lt. Edwin Lawrence Noble, was accepted just prior to his 28th birthday which occurred on August 23. Noble had been born in Charlestown, Massachusetts, and was a 1915 electrical engineering graduate of Yale University's Sheffield Scientific School. He enlisted in the U. S. Air Service in 1917, received his pilot's training at Mineola and was sent to France where he performed dependably without particular notoriety. Following the Armistice, he had remained in Europe with the A.E.F.'s Requisition and Claims Department where he first heard of the proposed Polish venture. Cooper and Fauntleroy hesitated in signing Noble as they had done with Clark, and for similar reasons. They were not sure of his flying ability; and his quiet, almost shy personality did not seem to fit the rugged assignment ahead. In the end they relented, and "Ig" Noble, as he came to be known, proved to be a good choice.

Completing the initial roster was Capt. Arthur H. Kelly, the lone non-pilot of the group. However, the slender Irishman from Virginia had had considerable combat exposure as

Lt. Carl Clark's uniform included a 1919 version of the historic four-cornered Polish military headgear, the ROGA-TYWKA. Tadeusz Kościuszko wore a similar cap more than a century earlier, a replica of which was included in the squadron's insignia.

a bombardier, aerial observer and navigator with the 96th U. S. Bombardment Squadron, having been credited with at least two German planes destroyed. Cooper who had known Kelly earlier, argued successfully that the project could use an officer of the latter's ability even though he had not had flight training.

And so the charter members of Cooper's and Fauntleroy's Polish expeditionary force were brought together and prepared (as well as they could be under the circumstances) for an unforeseeable adventure in an unfamiliar setting. It could easily have been said that they were brash and self-confident to believe that eight men could be a significant factor in a war which involved a million or more participants. After all, they didn't know what kind of airplanes—if any—would be available to them or where they would be stationed on the irregular, ill-defined thousand-mile front. There would be no brass bands to see them off. More than that, volunteer service such as they proposed was not widely popular, as the victorious Allied Powers gingerly approached the situation in eastern Europe, maneuvering and bargaining for a quick peace rather than continued conflict. In the United States, too, the idea of direct participation was not enthusiastically welcomed. Due primarily to the personal efforts of pianist Ignacy Jan Paderewski, the Polish cause generally received a sympathetic ear and moral support, but even the threat of international communism could not revive the hyper-patriotic spirit which had sent the A.E.F. to Europe in the first place. "Bring the boys home" was the joyous cry; a new age of peace and prosperity had dawned; it was time to put the uniforms away. Meanwhile, as French tailors measured Cooper, Fauntleroy and their new comrades for the blue attire of Gen. Józef Haller's Polish Army in exile, the eight young airmen—unlike the folks at home—were well aware that the pens at Versailles were not necessarily mightier than the swords in the borderlands between Poland and Russia.

While it was true that no trumpeters would be at the train station for their departure, the volunteers did not leave

Ignacy Jan Paderewski, famed pianist and Premier of Poland at the time, attended a farewell reception for the new Kościuszko Squadron at the Hotel Ritz in Paris. Gen. Tadeusz Rozwadowski (second from right), chief of the Polish Military Mission at the French capital, and Col. Harry Howland (right), U. S. military attache to the Poles, accompanied the Premier.

Paris totally without recognition or revelry. When their uniforms were completed and they had each been fitted with the rakish **rogatywka** the identifying Polish four-cornered military cap which dated back to Kościuszko's time), they were summoned to the Ritz Hotel for presentation to the Premier of Poland, the same Jan Paderewski, who had received such popular acclaim on his concert tours in the United States. In the hotel's Parisian Gardens the American officers were formally introduced to Paderewski by General Rozwadowski and Col. Harry Howland, U. S. military attache to the Polish Mission in France. As the ranking member of the honorees, Major Fauntleroy responded on behalf of his comrades, and then the Premier talked with each man individually and expressed his personal gratitude for the courageous undertaking to which they had committed themselves by written contract. In describing the farewell event, a newspaper reported:

> Major Fauntleroy in offering the services of himself and his men to Poland told the Premier that his pilots were all Americans, none of Polish blood, who came willingly to fight in the armies of the new sister republic of the United States against all enemies of Poland. Mr. Paderewski was visibly affected by Fauntleroy's words. "Nothing has ever touched me so much as the offer of you young men to fight and, if necessary, to die for my country," he said.

Even more noteworthy, however, the same news story referred to the unit as the Kościuszko Squadron, a designation to which Poles and Americans alike could ascribe the proper historical significance. The spirit of the unforgettable Polish patriot was resurrected by a handful of Yankees who took it upon themselves to repay a national favor owed to another volunteer just like themselves.

The settlement of the account was almost a century and a half overdue.

Meanwhile, there was one more party to attend. A lavish, liquid reception and dinner were arranged by General Rozwadowski at the Hotel Wagram. Prince Casimir Lubomirski, then Polish minister to the U. S., was a special guest, and the A.E.F. was represented by Colonel Howland and Gen. Ewing D. Booth, chief of staff. The drinks flowed freely, and in the toasting tradition for such occasions, empty wine glasses tinkled musically as they shattered in the fireplace.

It was truly a night to remember—although several of the celebrants had only hazy recollections of the party's end.

Chapter II

A Partnership of Eagles

Organizing the Kościuszko Squadron at a sidewalk cafe in Paris was one thing; getting the men to Warsaw was definitely another. Contrary to General Rozwadowski's original authorization letter, Clause 9 of the contract signed by the volunteers with the Polish government in France stipulated that the officers involved would pay their own way to and from Poland. As a result of his earlier agreement to serve Marshal Piłsudski's armed forces as a technical adviser, Major Fauntleroy had been given a ticket permitting him to travel in style by international express. The other members, however, were not that fortunate.

As enthusiastic as he was about the project, though, Captain Cooper was not about to let a small matter like troop logistics thwart his plan. With the help of Colonel Howland (who befriended the squadron in a variety of ways during its embryonic period), a transportation strategem was worked out, and on September 16, 1919, the seven officers—traveling incognito as Red Cross supply guards—left the Paris railway station on the first leg of their journey eastward in boxcar accommodations. At Coblenz they switched to an American Typhus Relief train, again with their ultimate mission and true ranks known to the two U. S. Medical Corps officers aboard, but **not** to the small squad of enlisted men in the health detachment.

At Coblenz the officers-in-disguise transferred to a U. S. Typhus Relief train for the remainder of the trip to Warsaw. (Left to right) Crawford, Cooper, Noble, Corsi and Kelly relaxed with Spad, their unofficial mascot, while a friendly goose kibitzed from above.

Enroute to their date with destiny, seven of the eight original Kościuszko Squadron airmen traveled incognito as Red Cross supply guards in a "sidedoor Pullman." Left to right are Corsi, Crawford, Shrewsbury, Clark, Kelly, Cooper (seated) and Noble.

It was hardly an auspicious beginning to their Polish odyssey. Dressed as privates in olive drab, the officers took their turns as kitchen police and listened silently (and sometimes angrily) as their doughboy hosts spoke with scorn about military aviators, who—one burly sergeant insisted—suffered most of their casualties falling down in the Paris subway between drunken parties. It wasn't always easy, but somehow the airmen-in-disguise maintained their composure and their secret as the train wheels click-clacked off the miles enroute to their date with destiny. Only Captain Cooper, an interminable pipe-smoker, experienced true suffering. Before the trip was over, he discovered that his comrades had given away dozens of cans from his personal tobacco supply which he had purchased in France to see him through the long winter. As the Coblenz-bound Red Cross train stopped at various way points enroute across Germany, crowds of local citizens had gathered around the rail car marked with an American flag and cheered happily as the generous soldiers tossed them the tins of Prince Albert which the beneficent donors thought were Red Cross give-away items. Later, when Cooper found his emptied sack, he raised his voice, too, but the resultant sound was not a joyful huzza!

———

Warsaw, the traditional capital of Poland, was not at all like Paris in the early autumn of 1919. The harsh visitations of war had taken an obvious toll, and—while much of the rest of the world was gaily celebrating the restoration of peace—the aged stronghold on the Vistula River continued to face the specter of renewed military involvement. When the train carrying the seven members of the Kościuszko Squadron arrived at the long sheds of the Vienna station on September 24, a sense of uneasiness prevailed in the city. Neither the Poles nor the Russian Reds were pursuing a vigorous campaign against one another at the time, and the vague prospects for the future contributed to the restless atmosphere among the people. As a matter of fact, secret negotiations for peace (which collapsed abortively on December 14) had been consented to separately by Marshal Piłsudski and by Vladimir Ilyich Ulynov, the founder of Bolshevik Communism best known by his pseudonym, Nikolay Lenin.

In Warsaw the American volunteers changed from their olive drab into the uniforms of Poland. They all wore a ROGATYWKA except Fauntleroy, who adopted one shortly afterwards. Left to right in the front row were: Shrewsbury, Noble, Crawford and Kelly; back: Clark, Fauntleroy, Cooper and Corsi.

Captain Cooper and his fellow volunteers had no way of knowing the current status of the war they came to fight, but after a week's confinement on a slow-moving train, they were ready for almost any kind of action. Before they left their sidedoor pullman, they changed from their nondescript OD's into the lake blue regalia of Polish military officers. Needless to say, the men of the typhus detachment were appropiately nonplussed when they learned who their traveling companions really were; the exulted airmen, on the other hand, wasted little time in retaliation for the verbal blasts and demeaning conditions imposed upon them during the trip. The wide-eyed, open-mouthed expressions on the faces of the medical relief crew constituted retribution enough.

Cooper's previous experience in the capital city greatly eased the arrival problems for the troupe of enthusiastic young officers who couldn't speak the language their uniforms represented. Quickly he arranged for horse-drawn cabs—picturesque Polish **dorożki**—to carry them across the war-emaciated metropolis to the Mokotów airdrome where they reported for duty, apparently to the dismay of the headquarters staff. Their presence, it seemed, added to the organizational confusion then faced by the Polish Air Force

The American volunteers signed a bilingual contract with the government of Poland for a term of six months and guaranteeing them "all the rights and privileges given to the Polish officers."

Shrewsbury Collection

Marshal Józef Piłsudski, Poland's Chief of State, was a fervent, strong-willed patriot whose leadership brought victory to his reborn nation against what seemed to be insurmountable odds. He personally greeted the Kościuszko pilots at Belvedere Palace when they arrived in Warsaw.

which was still in swaddling clothes and attempting desperately to make the giant leap from birthing to maturity in the space of a few short months. Although the officers had already signed contracts in Paris, a question arose over the possibility of diplomatic problems with the United States if one or more of the American citizens were killed. Another point of consideration was whether or not the volunteers should serve in a training capacity or be given front-line duty. Marshal Piłsudski's insistence that Poland could defeat her enemies without mercenaries was reiterated. Adding to the dilemma was the massive, complex task of building and equipping a cohesive, efficient military force from a melange of new draftees and the tens of thousands of returning Polish veterans from German, Austrian, Imperial Russian and other national armies.

In the meantime, the American volunteers were reunited with their commander, Major Fauntleroy, and assigned to temporary billeting in the Hotel Bristol at 42-44 Krakówskie Przedmiescie (Kraków Boulevard), Warsaw's most imposing thoroughfare. From this centrally located base, the young officers began their "last fling" sightseeing and entertainment sorties, the age-old custom of military personnel awaiting combat assignment. They visited **Stare Miasto,** the old town; sipped **miód,** the Polish spice-and-honey wine; toured historic attractions on both sides of the Vistula; and partied with other Americans then in the city—newsmen, Red Cross hostesses, diplomatic corps representatives and relief mission workers. They had such a good time, in fact, that Cooper later wrote: ". . . . my only fear was that half the squadron would be married before we could get away to the front."

During the period of anxious waiting, the Kościuszko Squadron was summoned to Belweder (Belvedere) Palace, the classic column-fronted governmental building at the southern end of Ujazdowskie Avenue where Józef Piłsudski, the 52-year-old head of the reborn Polish state, faced the enormous responsibilities of his historic role. Meeting the flint-hard

Marshal was a direct contrast to the earlier encounter with Premier Paderewski in Paris. Resplendent in their Haller blues, the volunteers reported to the spacious East Room of the 17th Century palace which had been reconstructed in 1822, five years after General Kościuszko's death. There Major Fauntleroy introduced his fellow officers to the one-time socialist revolutionary who, less than a year earlier, had been imprisoned in the German fortress at Magdeburg. Piłsudski listened intently to Fauntleroy's English words and the Polish translation which followed, but his rigid features behind a heavy, slightly graying mustache indicated neither a positive nor a negative reaction to the presentation.

The Marshal's reply—in deliberate, sharply enunciated words—was not at all like Paderewski's glowing tribute to their beneficent gesture. He [Piłsudski], as a 19th Century military traditionalist, still believed that battles had to be won by uniformed men, afoot or on horseback. Further, he was not yet convinced of the necessity for flying machines in warfare, and he was deeply concerned that the demands of movement and supply for aviation units would further complicate Poland's already serious logistical problems. Nonetheless, despite his somewhat divergent philosophy, the Polish leader—in his own way—was undoubtedly no less moved by the Kościuszko Squadron's acceptance of the Bolshevik challenge than Premier Paderewski had been a few weeks earlier. Possibly he saw in the young Americans something of the same spirit he himself had exhibited three decades before when he had been sentenced to exile in Siberia for his part in an anti-Tsarist plot. Through his interpreter he told them that if, under the circumstances, they were still willing to assume the responsibilities of their commitment to Poland, he would see to it that they were promptly assigned to an active air force unit. Then, with a snap of his heels and a quick salute, he turned and left the room.

———

Shortly after the appearance at Belvedere, the squadron's roster was increased to ten with the arrival of Lts. Edmund

Pike Graves and Elliott William Chess. Graves was born in Newburyport, Massachusetts, in 1891 and was a graduate of Harvard in the class of 1913. He enlisted in the British Royal Flying Corps, and after receiving pilot's wings in Canada, joined the training staff at the School of Aerial Gunnery in Fort Worth, Texas. Early in 1918 he was appointed instructor of acrobatics in the new School of Special Flying in Toronto, Canada. He was sent to England before the Armistice but never reached combat, and the disappointment ultimately led to his volunteering for the assignment in Poland.

Chess, a native of El Paso, Texas, also enlisted in the RFC while still a high school student. He likewise was trained in Canada and later saw service as a messenger pilot in England. He was still only 19 years old when he applied for acceptance in the Kościuszko Squadron, making him the youngest of the original ten members—all Americans, five from the U. S. Air Service, two from the British RFC/RAF and three with French military backgrounds (Fauntleroy having served in both the French Foreign Legion and the A.E.F.). Neither Graves nor Chess were known personally by the organization's founders, but they came to the unit on recommendation of friends in London. They were quickly assimilated into the group as charter members, however, and joined their fellow officers in the restless game of marking time until shipping orders arrived.

For Chess and Graves, the wait was relatively brief. They reported to the squadron on October 12, and four days later the official logbook of the Kościuszko Squadron recorded its first terse entry:

October 16: Left Warsaw, 10 p.m.

The second notation, equally as brief, marked the return of Captain Cooper to the City of the Lion in Galicia where he had witnessed the memorable examples of Polish courage which led, in time, to the creation of the volunteer unit. The daily log reported:

October 17: Arrived Lwów, 8:00 p.m.

In general, the military air service of resurgent Poland was created out of the scraps and pieces of World War I aviation surplus. Even for the long established nations, the development of personnel, equipment and flying techniques to wage war effectively from the sky had been a costly, trial-and-error process which was still largely in the experimental stage when the Armistice was declared. In slightly more than a decade after Wilbur and Orville Wright's first successful powered flight at Kitty Hawk, North Carolina, on December 17, 1903, heavier-than-air machines had been adapted by men to achieve destructive ends. In 1915 Anthony H. G. Fokker, a 25-year-old Dutch aircraft designer who had established a small factory near Berlin, perfected a synchronizing gear which permitted a machinegun to be fired through a revolving propeller without hitting it. His lethal idea transformed the airplane from a battle zone curiosity into a versatile device of warfare; and when the "new" Polish state came into being and had to begin immediately to protect herself on every side and from above, she, too, had to consider an air arm as part of her military preparation.

The establishment of the Polish Air Force was definitely not a simple, problem-less matter. There were too many priorities of equal or greater demand facing Marshal Piłsudski and his reborn nation. A solvent, functioning government was vital to continued existence. There were literally millions of hungry citizens to feed, some of them near starvation. The menace of typhus and other diseases growing out of the filth and famine of a long war was a stark reality. The hurried development of a traditional land army of infantry, cavalry and artillery — which Piłsudski personally comprehended — was of utmost importance for both internal and external needs. Consequently, from its birthing, the **Lotnictwo Wojskowa** (Military Aviation) was a needy, often misunderstood stepchild which survived to adulthood despite enormous odds.

Ironically enough, the majority of the pilots who came home to establish the Polish Air Force had been trained in

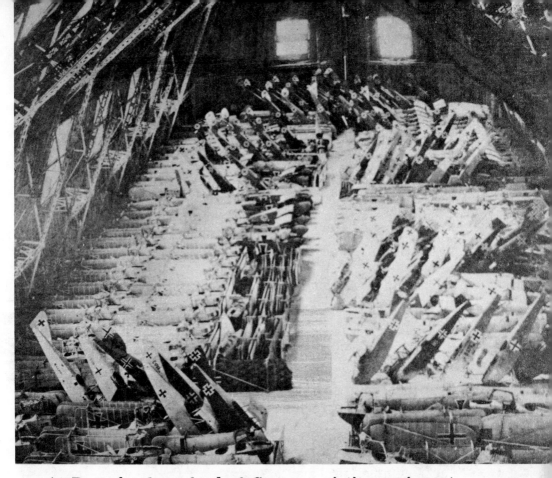

At Poznań a huge haul of German aviation equipment was found in a zeppelin hangar and commandeered. It was from such captured caches and scrap heaps that the Polish Air Force came into existence.

the service of the three partitioning powers: Germany, Austria and Russia. Their initial equipment also came from captured and abandoned airfields, a source of supply which had both good and bad features: it put them into business without a great monetary outlay, but it certainly gave them little choice of what they flew. At Rakowice airfield at Kraków some 40 Austrian aircraft were captured, half of which were Brandenburg trainers and the remaining divided between obsolete combat planes and derelict airframes. Partially trained Poles, with the help of friendly Hungarians, escaped from Hureczko field at Przemyśl and flew six additional Austrian planes to Rakowice (two others were destroyed by attacking Ukranians, two crashed enroute and two more were badly damaged in forced landings). At Lewandówka field near Lwów and the Lublin airdrome to the northwest, Polish patriots commandeered all available materiel left by the Austrians.

In the German portion of Poland, Mokotów field at Warsaw was peacefully evacuated, leaving to Piłsudski's forces a quantity of planes and other equipment which the Germans had earlier planned to fly out or destroy on the base. But the biggest haul was made at Ławica near Poznań where, in addition to other gear, Polish attackers took possession of a massive Zeppelin hangar which contained scores of engineless airframes of varied makes and condition. Between 200 and 250 planes capable of flying or with potentially high salvage value were taken in reclaimed Polish territories in the final two months of 1918. Jerzy B. Cynk in his **History of the Polish Air Force** described most of the captured machines as obsolete or of poor quality — but, more than that, they consisted of a mechanical hodgepodge of some 40 different fuselage styles and at least 35 assorted types of engines.

Out of this jumble of odds and ends, then, the Polish military air service emerged, due in large measure to the dedication and doggedness of the men involved. Though many of them were Russian-trained and had no experience with German or Austrian planes, they learned (often by costly error) to fly anything and everything. If there were no spare parts available, they created them or found some alternate way to make the machines serviceable. Even Marshal Piłsudski and the "old guard" ground fighters had to be impressed by the early accomplishments of the young air-minded patriots, some of whom participated heroically and effectively in the liberation of Lwów from the Ukranians, and all of whom were eager to become part of the 20 Polish combat squadrons (of 15 planes each) which were envisioned in the 1920 national armament plan.

Among the units already in existence when the government program was being finalized was the Seventh Fighter Squadron which had grown out of the aeronautical rubble at Kraków in November of 1918. The Third Combat Squadron, as it was originally designated, was rushed from Rakowice field to the defense of Lwów virtually on a "grow as you fight" basis. One of the charter members, Lt. Aleksander Seńkowski, a navigator who became a pilot while serving with the unit, described the impoverished beginning:

> The equipment of the squadron was very poor. It possessed only old-type Brandenburg planes with Austro-Daimler engines of 160 horsepower, and one antique OeFFAG 51, nicknamed "Bocian," [The Stork] . . . . [We] did not have a single lorry and later received only one passenger car. Equipment consisted of a box of old-fashioned tools and a few barrels of gasoline. Thus equipped, the squadron started to move toward the battle in Lwów. The planes flew and the equipment went by train.

Despite their multiple limitations, the pioneer Polish airmen attacked Ukrainian ground troops in their rickety two-seaters, with a navigator in each plane firing an infantry-type Schwarzlose machinegun over the side of the cockpit as effectively as he could with the fabric ammunition belt flapping in the air currents. There were no special devices for the ejection of bombs (also surplus items from Russia and Austria). "The lighter bombs were thrown by hand and the heavier ones were pushed through the navigator's door," Lieutenant Seńkowski recalled.

In the spring of 1919 three Fokker E.V fighter planes arrived to upgrade the Seventh Squadron's combat equipment, and during the summer — while Cooper and Fauntleroy were busily rounding up recruits in Paris — a dozen

Prior to the arrival of the American volunteers, the pilots of the Seventh Squadron were Poles who had trained and seen service in the armed forces of several different countries. When Major Fauntleroy took over from Lieutenant Rayski (front center), three other officers from this group remained with the unit: Lieutenant Idzikowski (second from left, rear), Lieutenant Weber (right rear) and Lieutenant Konopka (second from right, front).

Lt. Ludomił Rayski (center), relinquished command of the Polish Seventh Squadron to Major Fauntleroy. Rayski later was to head the entire Polish Air Force and to become involved in a major controversy regarding World War II preparedness. With him in winter flying gear were Captain Cooper (left) and Lieutenant Graves.

Albatros D.IIIs were assigned to the unit, then taking advantage of the reduced troop activity to improve its fighting capabilities in terms of both men and machines.

The Seventh Squadron was under the command of Lt. Ludomił Rayski (later to become commander-in-chief of the entire Polish Air Force) when the train from Warsaw arrived in Lwów on October 17 with its ten new replacement officers. On the 18th, Lieutenant Rayski was succeeded by Major Fauntleroy, and the unit's numerical designation was supplanted by the name of the Polish national hero the American volunteers had come to repay. The **Eskadra Kościuszkowska** — a partnership of eagles — was no longer a visionary idea, and if Captain Cooper experienced an inward glow of pride when he saw Polish and American pilots shaking hands to pledge their mutual commitment as flying comrades, he had sufficient justification for the feeling.

Chapter III

The First Casualty: A Symbolic Gesture

Maj. Cedric Errol Fauntleroy, first commander of the Kościuszko Squadron under its new designation, was born at Fayette, Jefferson County, Mississippi, on November 22, 1891. His Huguenot ancestors in France originally bore the name Font-le-roi (Fountain of the King) which was Anglecized after the family migrated to England as a result of the religious rebellion in their homeland. A later generation of Fauntleroys heeded the lure of the American colonies and settled in Virginia. With the passage of time, Major Fauntleroy's grandfather — Franklin B. — moved westward where he established a small plantation northeast of Natchez.

The major's father — William James Fauntleroy —served as a Texas Ranger, according to family lore, after which he settled down on the family farm which had been severely impoverished as a result of the Civil War. Young Cedric attended the Catholic Brothers School in Natchez until he was 14, and then he, too, succumbed to the traditional Fauntleroy affinity for geographic mobility. By his own admission, he ran away from home to follow the cattle herds of Texas as a transient cowboy. Following that experience, he roamed from job to job and from place to place, working for a time as a machinist for the Missouri Pacific Railroad at Ferriday, Louisiana, and McGehee, Arkansas. Ultimately he arrived in Chicago where he found employment as an auto-

Maj. Cedric E. Fauntleroy—former cowboy, railroad machinist and auto mechanic—was co-founder of the Kościuszko Squadron and its first commander. The native Mississippian had been a member of the French Foreign Legion before he transferred to the Air Section of the A.E.F. where he served primarily as a test pilot.

mobile mechanic. In a reminiscent interview many years later, Fauntleroy told of his somewhat emotional turn to a military career:

When the war came along . . . . and the **Lusitania** was sent down by the Germans, I became infuriated over the fact that Americans no longer had the right to travel on the high seas, so I began to look for some way of retaliation if

the government . . . . didn't see fit to do anything about it . . . . I finally wound up in the
French Foreign Legion. I paid my own way to
France. I had one suit of clothes and two changes
of underwear because I realized that I would be
in the service and civilian clothes were no longer
required.

When the United States finally entered the war, Fauntleroy transferred to the Air Section of the A.E.F. where he
qualified for pilot's training at Issoudon. His brief acquain-
tance there with Merian Cooper was the beginning of the
fateful chain of events which, less than two years later,
brought him to Lwów where he assumed command of the
Kościuszko Squadron. In addition to the nine Americans who
arrived with him, the roster of the unit included six Polish
officers: Lieutenant Rayski, a Pole of Turkish citizenship
who was born at Kraków in 1892, studied engineering at the
technical university in Lwów and learned to fly in the Turkish Air Force under German officers during World War I;
Capt. Zbigniew Orzechowski (the squadron's non-flying adjutant); Lt. Władysław Konopka and Lt. Aleksander Seńkowski, who had each served previously under the Austrian
flag; Lt. Jerzy A. Weber (whose mother was Chinese) and
Lt. Ludwik Idzikowski, former pilots of the Imperial Russian
Air Service. Captain Cooper may have had the basic idea
which brought such a heterogeneous group of men together,
but the responsibility for welding them into a spirited, pro-
ficient and aggressive combat squadron was placed square-
ly on the broad shoulders of the former military test pilot
from Mississippi.

Fauntleroy had had enough command experience to know
that his first task was to assess the quantity and quality of
the personnel and equipment under his charge. He and Cooper had discussed the individual talents and potential liabilities
of the American pilots. He recognized that their overall combat flying time during World War I was somewhat limited,

but he was also realist enough to understand that "making up for what they missed" was one of the unmentioned reasons why several of them signed their contracts.

The enlisted men — ground crew members, orderlies and administrative NCOs — were, like the Polish officers carried over from the Seventh Squadron, largely veterans of the armed forces of the three partitioning powers. Dealing with them involved a language barrier which was sure to be an aggravation — at least for a time — but with interpreters and a Babel-mixture of French, German, Russian, Polish and English, the major was relatively confident that the communications obstacle could be surmounted. Another slight concern was familiarizing the men with "the American way of doing things" — the less formal adherence to military discipline and the direct approach taken by the Yankee officers when a problem needed solving.

Lewandówka airdrome, the Kościuszko Squadron's first home, was situated on a slightly elevated plain in the western outskirts of Lwów. The field itself was a mile wide and almost two miles long. A covering of soft, white beach-type

Members of the Polish ground crew were heroes in anonymity of the Kościuszko Squadron story. In general, they overcame serious language barriers and lack of training to serve their pilots well. Shrewsbury Collection

sand provided a level takeoff and landing surface, but it could be a boon or a burden, depending upon how a pilot touched down the wheels of his plane. Hangar facilities were adequate but not fancy, and the main rail line leading into the city from the west passed between the field and the Lwów Air Park, the principal repair station for all squadrons serving the Galician sector. The rail siding was ideal for developing the organization's mobile ground-support train, a concept which Cooper and Fauntleroy fostered to keep the Kościuszko pilots constantly within flying range of the front line, no matter how fluid the latter might be.

As for aircraft, the supply situation was adequate but not rosy. The old Brandenburg C.Is and Fokker E.Vs were still functioning, but the primary planes in which the unit would make or break its early reputation were the Albatros D.IIIs which the Seventh Squadron acquired while the American officers were still in Paris.

The fighter planes at Lwów had been built by the Oesterreichische Flugzeugfabric A. G. (OeFFAG) for the Austrian Air Service and were cigar-shaped single-seaters with a fuselage of laminated wood. Their Austro-Daimler engines had a range of 185 to 225 horsepower (depending on the series number) and a maximum speed of 122 miles per hour. They were capable of climbing to a thousand meters (3,280 feet) in 3.3 minutes and had a two-hour flying endurance. The D.IIIs were 24 feet, 5/8th of an inch long, with a wing span of 29 feet, 8¼ inches. Twin fixed eight millimeter Schwarzlose machineguns, firing through the revolving propellor arc at approximately 100 rounds a minute, provided the standard armament.

The first D.IIIs, produced by the Ostdeutsche Albatros Werke at Schneidemühl in the German section of Poland, were introduced to German fighter pilots in January of 1917, so the design style was somewhat dated by the time the Seventh Polish Squadron received its initial Albatros shipment in August of 1919. Baron Manfred von Richthofen, the noted German ace, flew one of the first D.IIIs in combat, but when

Albatros D.IIIs, marked with Polish chessboard and Kościuszko Squadron emblems, were the first planes flown by the American pilots in the service of Poland. Powered by Austro-Daimler engines, they were armed with twin fixed eight millimeter Schwarzlose machineguns geared to fire between the revolving propeller blades.

he noticed a threatening crack in its lower wing during a dogfight, he landed quickly and thereafter flew other makes of planes until the structural deficiency of the Albatros was corrected to his satisfaction. The same day von Richthofen switched machines — January 24, 1917 — two other German pilots were killed because of the fatal weakness of the early D.IIIs.

Chapter III

During the month which followed their arrival in Lwów, the Americans flew the unfamiliar planes whenever the weather permitted. Mishaps were minor because the flyers (except for one wild acrobatic sortie by Lieutenant Graves) were relatively cautious as they adjusted to the handling characteristics of their strange craft. Lieutenant Rayski had told Major Fauntleroy that the Albatros **probably** wouldn't nose over when landing in the soft sand — but he added the slightly ominous suggestion that it might be a good idea to bring it down quite tail high and to turn off the ignition when the wheels hit the ground as a precaution against fire, just in case a flip occurred. Rayski's remarks were generally well heeded because nobody wanted to be the first to crack up a squadron plane, no matter what its vintage or performance potential.

When the weather kept them on the ground, the men turned their attention to outfitting their airdrome-on-wheels, the rail cars which were to give the unit logistical self-sufficiency wherever it might move. There were many leisure hours, too, and the pilots were generously wined and dined by Lwówians and personnel of the American Red Cross which had its local headquarters at Potocki Palace. On the night of November 21, a party was held in the ancient aristocratic abode as a prelude to a gala civic celebration planned for the following day. Marshal Piłsudski was to appear as the major feature of the event organized to commemorate the liberation of Lwów from Ukranian occupation a year earlier. As part of the festivities, the Kościuszko Squadron was ordered to provide an aerial escort and to perform a flying exhibition for the Chief of State who would be reviewing troops from a festooned stand on St. Mary's Square.

Though the squadron had been socked in by the weather during the previous 24 hours, Saturday, November 22, dawned bright and clear. By coincidence it was Major Fauntleroy's 28th birthday, and obviously it would be a memorable one, even though he was not to be the guest of honor. According

Early in November four members of the Boys' Legion who had fought in the defense of Lwów against the Ukrainians were dinner guests of the squadron. Pictured with the decorated young heroes were Fauntleroy, Corsi, Cooper, Kelly and Rayski.

to plan, he would lead a six-man flight — consisting of officers Corsi, Idzikowski, Konopka, Chess and Graves — over the parade route following a telephone signal from Lieutenant Noble, who was strategically located at the railroad station where he could see the line of march. Also as part of the show, Captain Cooper, with the squadron adjutant as observer, was to fly a lone pass-over in one of the Brandenburgs.

First casualty of the squadron was Lt. Edmund P. Graves, who crashed to his death during an aerial exhibition at Lwów on November 22, 1919. A former instructor in flight acrobatics, Graves apparently put too much stress on his Albatros and the top wing buckled.

As it turned out, Marshal Piłsudski had to cancel his appearance, but the celebration went on as announced. When the call came from the railroad station, the planes took off to begin their ceremonial flight in the traditional, picturesque V formation. Thousands of Polish necks were craned skyward as the geometric pattern passed overhead. Then, as the squadron completed its run and swung in a wide arc to return to the reviewing stand area, three planes — piloted by Fauntleroy, Corsi and Graves — peeled off to present the scheduled stunting exhibition. Cheers of admiration rose from the street below as the skilled flyers accomplished a series of maneuvers in unison and then broke formation to perform individually. As Fauntleroy and Corsi climbed to higher altitudes to give themselves more operating room, Lieutenant Graves — the fearless one and former instructor of aerial acrobatics — abruptly turned his plane upside down and flew directly over the reviewing stand. The startling effect on the crowd was what he undoubtedly expected it would be, and it became quite clear that Graves was going to take advantage of a big audience to demonstrate his flying ability. Unfortunately, as he reached the vicinity of Potocki Palace, he apparently tried to force his overworked Albatros through a fast double roll, and a sharp gasp arose from the viewers as the upper wing buckled and dropped down on the lower span on the left side of the ship, tearing it away. From an altitude of little more than 200 feet, the 28-year-old daredevil plummeted to his death.

The errant Albatros crashed into the roof of the palace where the night previously Edmund Pike Graves had enjoyed the food and festivities with his fellow officers. The resultant fire burned the upper portion of the building as Red Cross workers scurried to save what furnishings and supplies they could. Meanwhile, Lieutenant Noble gathered the lifeless body of the former British RFC/RAF flyer into the squadron automobile and began the sad ride back to Lewandówka field.

Two days later the funeral of the first member of the Kościuszko Squadron to die for the cause of Poland was held at the Evangelical Church in Lwów, and though Lieutenant Graves never lived to face the enemy, his death was recognized as a symbol of the total dedication of the Americans to their voluntary commitment. An eyewitness account described details of the stirring event:

> . . . . His companions then carried the casket, covered with the American and Polish flags, accompanied by the tolling of bells and the mournful chords of funeral marches. Above the retinue circled a plane piloted by a Polish flyer [Lt. Franciszek Peter of the Sixth Squadron] who was accompanying his friend on the road to his final resting place. A company of General Haller's blue-garbed men, armed with bayonets,

marched at the head of the funeral cortege. They were followed by a platoon of the Seventh Flight Squadron bearing the name of Tadeusz Kościuszko in which Lieutenant Graves had served. Next came a military band followed by those bearing an endless number of wreathes, a veritable kaleidoscope of flowers, verdure and national colors. The first wreath was a huge offering from the officers of the Seventh Squadron. It was woven around an airplane propellor.

.... The rest followed in this order: from the command of the Third Flight Group, from the Officers' Corps, from the French Mission, from the Sentry Battalion, and so many, many more. Three ministers preceded the coffin. Three pairs of horses pulled the unusual caisson accorded only to a pilot killed in action: an airplane decorated with fir branches .... Crowds lining both sides of the street gazed at the procession. The retinue came down the streets named Zielona, Pańska and Piekarska toward the Cemetery of the Defenders of Lwów. Even the street lights were covered with mourning crepe.

Some time after the interment, the other pilots of the squadron gathered in the officers' mess at the small red brick building on the airfield. In customary fashion they toasted their missing comrade represented by his empty chair at the table. On the following morning, however, the chair was gone, in keeping with another tradition of combat airmen — never to brood over the passing of a fellow participant in an inherently dangerous and unpredictable occupation.

————

At 5:15 on the morning after Lieutenant Graves' funeral, a kitchen orderly went to the garage to get some gasoline to start the fire for breakfast. Whether the cause was a candle he carried (as the logbook indicated) or a cigarette he carelessly smoked (as several of the officers contended), the explosive result was an engulfing blaze which destroyed the squadron's horses, carriages and two automobiles before it was brought under control. The orderly himself escaped with head and facial burns, but the second tragic event in four days was a disturbing blow to the unit which was just beginning to function as a cohesive entity.

Lieutenant Graves' funeral was a solemn event in Lwów. The cortege included a plane fuselage bedecked with fir branches on which the coffin rested (center of picture). Flying comrades of the dead officer followed bareheaded directly behind the unusual caisson.

Corsi Collection

The day was not a total loss, however, because it brought to the squadron a pint-sized visitor from Wilmington, North Carolina, who wasted no time expressing his desire to join the organization. Harmon Chadbourn Rorison, a five-foot, five-inch former American Air Service pilot with the demeanor of a bantam rooster, had paid his own expenses to Lwów to sign on with the Kościuszko volunteers he had heard about when he returned to the United States. A 1916 graduate of the University of Georgia, Rorison had taken private flying lessons before his enlistment, and like several other members of the unit, he had trained at Mineola and Issoudon before being assigned to combat duty with the 22nd Aero Squadron. He knew what it meant to confront an enemy in the air, and on one sortie near Beaumont, France, on November 3, 1918, he had achieved a triple kill which was described in the official citation which accompanied a Distingished Service Cross:

> While on a bombing mission with 5 other pilots, his patrol was attacked by 18 enemy planes (type Fokker). Three of his comrades were immediately shot down, but he continued in the fight for 30 minutes and destroyed 2 Fokkers which were attacking the other 2 members of his patrol. With his plane badly damaged and himself wounded, he succeeded in shooting down another Fokker just before 1 of his guns was put out of action. By skillful maneuvering he shook off the rest of the Fokkers and reached his lines, 15 miles away, in safety.

With credentials like that Lieutenant Rorison was a welcome replacement for Lieutenant Graves, and Major Fauntleroy immediately sent the sandy-haired Tarheel to Warsaw for official assignment. By November 30 the new officer was back at Lewandówka, properly enrolled and ready for his first turn in an Albatros.

Captain Corsi (left) and Captain Cooper were appointed commanders of the two squadron flight units, designated "Kościuszko" and "Pulaski." Wet and muddy Lewandówka field at Lwów typified the continuing weather problems faced by the flyers.

Before Rorison's arrival, Fauntleroy had divided the squadron into two flights, "Pulaski" commanded by Captain Cooper and "Kościuszko" led by Captain Corsi. The new officer was assigned to the former along with Konopka, Rayski, Crawford and Kelly. Corsi's flyers included Clark, Weber, Seńkowski, Idzikowski, Noble and Chess. To assist in identifying the planes of the two flights, the noses of the machines under Captain Cooper were painted bright red and those under Captain Corsi a distinct blue. But even more important, the squadron itself finally got an appropriate insignia to distinguish its aircraft from all others in the Polish Air Force.

Lieutenant Chess (whose name was informally Polonized to Chesski by his fellow officers) was the design artist.

Beginning with some casual doodling on the back of a menu at the Hotel Georgę in Lwów, the young Texan had developed the red, white and blue escutcheon which combined symbolic elements of Tadeusz Kościuszko's service at home and abroad. Thirteen stars and thirteen stripes represented the American colonies, and superimposed were the Polish leader's historically familiar red velvet four-cornered cap and two scimitar-like scythe blades with which peasant patriots under Kościuszko had battled Poland's enemies in the past. When it was completed, the unique insignia was emblazoned on the fuselages of the squadron's planes as a proud mark of distinction. It complemented the red-and-white chessboard symbol which appeared on the wings and rudders of all Polish machines, the latter design — according to aviation historian Jerzy Cynk — having been the personal plane marking of Lt. Stefan Stec, who also had commanded the Seventh Squadron prior to the arrival of the Americans. During the Ukranian campaign Lieutenant Stec, in a Fokker E.V, had attacked and shot down an enemy Nieuport, a feat which was recorded as the first dogfight between single-seaters won by a Polish Air Force pilot.

So the Kościuszko Squadron had a tradition and a trademark to go with the tragedy of Lieutenant Graves' untimely death. Understandably, the restless young officers were beginning to chafe at the joy-stick for combat action. They had signed up to fight Bolsheviks, and they were ready!

Chapter IV

Winter Calm Before the Springtime Storm

The year 1919 was a time of paradox. Supposedly, peace had returned to a battle-weary world, and — in the United States especially — an almost frantic effort was made to escape from war and its vestiges as quickly as possible. The dismantling of the American Expeditionary Force was almost a head-over-heels operation. In its final edition on June 13, 1919, **The Stars and Stripes,** official publication of the A.E.F., noted that 1,322,971 officers and men had already been hurried homeward and that a race was on to complete the job by August. A limited occupation force, some specialty troops and less than 1,000 relief administration personnel were to be left behind to tie down the loose ends and to get Europe started on the road to recovery.

Unfortunately, it was not as simple as that. America's buoyant spirit of optimism was not enough to overcome the realities which existed where armies had marched back and forth across the land for more than four years, leaving slow-healing wounds and a survival-conscious populace. More than that, though, the emergence of Red Russia — with the grandiose revolutionary goals of her leaders — was a specter which precluded belief by central and eastern Europeans in the slogan (so popular in the United States) that "the war to end all wars" was over.

Both sides used armored trains (like this Russian rail unit) throughout the war. Of varied and strange design, the trains often housed command headquarters and were therefore prime targets for aerial attack.

Beginning in 1903, a philosophical split had developed in the five-year-old Russian Social-Democratic Labour Party. In simple terms, the left wing headed by Lenin advocated a disciplined, proletariat-dominated, centralized organization, while the right wing — to which Lev Davidovich Bronstein (Leon Trotsky) then adhered — urged a more extensive membership and a role of authority for the bourgeoisie in the expected revolution. In the party congress of 1903 the left wingers prevailed and were called **bolsheviks** ("those of

A squadron line-up in front of their aircraft in late 1919 at Lwów. Left to right they are Rayski, Kelly, Cooper, Orzechowski, Konopka, Chess, Fauntleroy, Weber, Seńkowski, Noble, Corsi, Shrewsbury and Idzikowski.

the majority") as opposed to the **mensheviks** ("those of the minority"). In time the term Bolshevik became a popular synonym for all Communists.

From the Polish point of view, however, it made little difference what terminology was used. The threat of incursion by Russia — whether Tsarist or Marxist — was an age-old fear. Bolshevism, on the other hand, added a new dimension of concern to Marshal Piłsudski and his struggling government. Not only did Poland have to be prepared for a military invasion from the east, but the prospects of internal revolt — the seeds of which were carefully nurtured by Communist agents among the Polish workers — made it mandatory for the reborn nation to maintain a greater emphasis on the swords of war rather than on the plowshares of peace.

So it was that the Kościuszko Squadron had a necessity for being. The American pilots and their Polish comrades assumed that sooner or later they would come to grips with the Bolsheviks (whom they derisively referred to as Bolos), but in the meantime, a seemingly interminable period of waiting and wondering prevailed. The news out of Russia was sketchy and often contradictory. No one knew when or where the Reds would strike against Poland, if indeed they would strike at all. The counter revolutionary forces of Deniken (in the Ukraine), General Nikolai Yudenich (out of Estonia) and Admiral Alexander Visilevich Kolchak (in Siberia) — not to mention hunger, typhus, desertion and intra-party dissention — kept the Bolshevik hierarchy so engrossed that a respite on the Polish front was a temporary blessing.

Meanwhile, in the giant international chess game of diplomacy, the proposals, bargains, compromises, leverages and assorted maneuvers were so complex that even the participants seemed, at times, to be confused. In America President Wilson tried desperately — at the cost of his life, ultimately — to convince Congress, through public opinion, that his peace proposals deserved acceptance. Concurrently, the United States exhibited considerable reluctance to become re-involved in Europe over the fate of Poland. At the same time Great Britain was even more averse to a Polish-Russian confrontation and attempted to apply strong pressures on Piłsudski's government to force a settlement of the border question whether the results were favorable to the Poles or not. Winston Churchill seemed convinced that Bolshevism would collapse quickly under the weight of its own absurdity, and David Lloyd George, the British prime minister, reputedly had jeered: "What can you expect of a country that sends a pianist to a peace conference?" Only France of the victorious powers responded with a measure of generosity to the Polish needs for war material, but even the French were less concerned about Poland's national fulfillment than they were over the fact that a Bolshevik victory there would unite Russian workers with the German proletariat, and after that the revolution would surely extend its malignancy westward across the Rhine.

Flying open cockpit air-planes in the cold of winter over Poland required heavy garb as worn by Major Fauntleroy. The pilots also coated their f a c e s with grease or Vaseline.

The men at Lewandówka airdrome were warriors with-out war. Moreover, the snow and cold of the early Galician winter added to their restlessness by keeping them out of the air for extended periods. The squadron logbook for the month of December, for instance, carried a brief "no flying" entry for 21 of the 31 days. In a letter home, Lieutenant Noble told of his personal efforts to keep busy:

An English major told me that he would try to get a pair of skis for me in Vienna, and I hope to have some skiing to pass away the time when the weather is too bad for flying. I wish that you would send me a punching-bag and swivel, such as I used to have in the barn. I could rig it up in the hangar.

The Yuletide brought a welcome diversion for the grounded pilots. A fir tree was appropriately decorated in the mess hall; candles burned brightly in cartridge-case sconces fastened to the wall; and on Christmas Eve a gala party included a good-luck visit by the traditional Polish chimney sweep. A hand-crank phonograph provided the music, and the squadron's friends from the American Red Cross added to the occasion with gifts of candy and tobacco. On December 25 the log recorded that a nine-course dinner — featuring turkey and white bread — was a highlight of the holiday season.

American Red Cross women stationed at Lwów helped brighten the long winter hours at Lewandówka Field for the frustrated Kościuszko flyers.

Corsi Collection

Miss Ellen Thorson from North Dakota, one of the American Red Cross workers in Poland, was garbed in furs for a cold winter flight with Captain Corsi.

Only two of the officers, Crawford and Shrewsbury, missed the festivities. They had been sent by rail to Kamenets Podolski to see if a cache of aviation supplies taken from the Austrians there was of any value to the squadron. They were also instructed to reconnoiter possible flying fields in the vicinity in case the unit would be ordered to that area. In the Ukranian city, the two American flyers in Polish uniforms became increasingly aware of the Bolshevik propaganda efforts among the workers, many of whom greeted them sullenly and suspiciously at every turn. It was difficult to know, of course, whether the Ukranians (and some of the resident Poles) were converts to Communism, whether they feared the Russian Cheka (the Extraordinary Commission for Combating Counter-revolution and Sabotage), or whether they were merely so tired of the ebb and flow of Austrians, Whites, Reds, nationalists and pillaging partisans that they no longer trusted anyone.

On January 7 Lieutenants Noble and Rorison were sent to relieve Crawford and Shrewsbury at Kamenets Podolski. Meanwhile, the squadron members at Lwów watched snow, rain and sleet fall almost steadily for 12 consecutive days. The effect on morale was understandable, and Fauntleroy had his hands full keeping his keyed-up flyers relatively civil. In a reminiscent interview more than four decades later, he recalled:

> Everybody got into everybody else's hair, and they got to fighting and quarreling among themselves. I said to Cooper one day . . . . "Look, if I'm going to run this outfit, I'm going to run it like an army outfit, and the first guy that gives me any back-talk, I'm going to throw in the brig." He said, "That's all right with me" — and that's what I did!

The best antidote for the pilots' "cabin fever" was action, of course, but the weather and the high commands of both Polish and Bolshevik forces seemed to conspire against the squadron. The men flew training and familiarization missions whenever they could, and at least twice the rumored approach of enemy aircraft proved to be a false alarm as the D.IIIs roared out to do battle and came back untested. On one occasion an unidentified plane was actually sighted, but it turned out to be an off-course Polish two-seater from another squadron.

To break the monotony, there were several trips — by plane and by rail — to Warsaw and other cities in pursuit of unanswered requisitions for supplies and rations, and during the hiatus, Lieutenant Chess, in another burst of creativity, accomplished a particularly worthwhile achievement. As he tinkered with the synchronizing gear for the machineguns on his plane, he found a way to double the firing speed, an innovation for which he and his fellow officers would be extremely grateful in the months ahead.

While the majority of the pilots fretted and fussed in the red brick operations building at Lewandówka field, Lieutenant Noble had moved from Kamenets Podolski to Husiatyn, some 35 miles to the north on the Zbrucz River. From there, in another letter dated January 20, 1920, he described his mission and the conditions under which he lived:

> I have just arrived in this place, which used to be a city but which is now nothing but a heap of broken brick. I have been sent here to take charge of transporting some captured aviation material into Poland, and with my orderly and interpreter am living in what was formerly a private car of some Russian. Of course now it is in rather poor condition — no heat and no light but plenty of lice . . . . It is snowing and rather cold but we manage to keep fairly warm. Food is mighty scarce and the main supply is black bread and tea . . . . It is impossible to buy anything here and all I have for baggage is my blanket, gun and a couple of books. I am expecting another officer soon and I hope that he brings some supplies. I have my pipe, a bit of tobacco, a candle and my two books on electricity, and the two soldiers have a bottle of volnay, which is nearly 100% alcohol and which they seem to take a nip of now and then with great delight, although after I tried it I was afraid to breathe near the candle for fear of exploding . . .

On January 28 the squadron finally received an official assignment, and though it did not include direct contact with the enemy, the mission was welcomed with such an enthusiastic response that it almost resulted in a seemingly contagious comedy of errors. To thwart Bolshevik interception

Speaks Collection

Lt. Elliott Chess, bundled up in winter gear, was the youngest pilot in the Kościuszko organization. He was credited with designing the squadron emblems, re-setting the synchronization gears to double the firing speed of the machineguns on the D.IIIs and bending the vanes on bombs so they would "scream" as they fell.

Lieutenant Chess was credited with designing the squadron insignia on the back of a menu card at the Hotel George in Lwów. The 13 stars and 13 stripes represented the original colonies of the United States. The four-cornered cap—a replica of Tadeusz Kościuszko's red velvet ROGATYWKA—was superimposed over crossed scythes with which Polish peasants of an earlier generation fought invading Russians.

of telegraph communications, a courier was requested to deliver important messages to the advance base of the Polish forces at Tarnopol, some 80 miles east of Lwów, and Lieutenant Chess was given the responsibility for carrying the metal tube full of orders through the biting sub-zero temperatures to the outpost. Actually it was so bitterly cold that the squadron mechanics had difficulty warming up the motor of Chess's plane. Finally, however, the machine was declared ready; the pilot greased his face heavily to protect himself against frost bite; the blocks were pulled; and the Albatros sputtered into the frigid air.

Only a few minutes had elapsed when the lieutenant heard his Austro-Daimler engine cough and begin to lose power. When he realized that his plane simply wasn't going to make it, Chess kicked the rudder hard and headed back to Lewandówka. As he approached the airfield the motor quit entirely, and the young Texan rode his ship in for an almost successful dead-stick landing—until he hit a patch of ice and skidded into an encrusted snow bank which flipped the Albatros completely over.

Frustrated and irate—with his nose bleeding profusely from the impact—Lieutenant Chess burrowed out of the drift with the dispatch tube in his hand and angrily demanded another plane in which to complete his mission. No one wanted to challenge him in the mood he was in, so a second D.III was readied and soon he was back in the air heading eastward. This time the water with which a thoughtless mechanic had filled the radiator froze solid almost immediately and Chess found himself enroute to Tarnopol with a red hot engine. Almost miraculously, though, he arrived over the airfield safely, only to land the plane in a heavy blanket of snow more than wheel deep and into which the propeller of the nose-heavy Albatros quickly imbedded itself. To his chagrin and embarrassment, for the second time in a single day, Lieutenant Chess completed another unceremonious half somersault.

To add to the excitement, Captain Cooper became concerned when Chess took off with temper flaring after the first

Kościuszko pilots were often called upon to deliver messages to ground units. Orders were dropped in cylindrical tubes such as the one shown here by Captain Corsi.

accident, so he climbed into a plane and followed the lieutenant just in case something else happened. It did—only Cooper was the victim. A few miles out of Lwów, the metal cowling over the D.III's engine broke loose and slammed back against the plane's upper wing, cutting off Cooper's vision and threatening to do additional damage to the craft and possibly to the pilot himself if it flipped back onto the cockpit. By skillful maneuvering, however, the veteran flyer reversed his direction and worked his way back to the airdrome where he, too, severely ruffled the plywood feathers of still another Albatros in a blind, splintering crash-landing. For the Kościuszko Squadron it had not been what anybody could justifiably call a fruitful day!

Unfortunately, January 29 did not bring an end to the vexating streak of bad luck. Temperatures had not improved, and that morning Captain Corsi donned the furs and greased up to make the next courier flight. Again the mechanics had difficulty warming up the plane which had its tail skid propped on an upturned gas drum while a young crewman held down on the metal runner to keep the blocked-up machine from nosing over when the rpm's were increased. It wasn't long before the continuing back-lash of flesh-numbing air from the propeller took its toll on the ill-clad soldier. He released his grasp momentarily to cover his freezing ears and in an instant the plane's tail flipped up—and one more Albatros was temporarily out of commission. The mission had to be flown, however, so Corsi borrowed a red-nosed D.III from Cooper's Pulaski flight and without further trouble managed to get away to the first of two dispatch drops. He found the isolated outpost easily, jettisoned the proper message tube to arm-waving troops below and then proceeded on to Tarnopol.

As Corsi cruised almost leisurely toward his destination, the weather changed suddenly and strong winds began to buffet the plane from the northwest. The accompanying heavy snowfall added to his difficulties and made it impossible for him to maintain his bearings. Just before his gasoline supply was exhausted, the storm let up enough for him to spot a small clearing in the wooded terrain and skillfully he brought the Albatros down parallel to the furrows in the roughly plowed field. But his problems had just begun. Almost immediately a soldier emerged from the trees, firing his rifle spasmodically as he ran toward the plane. Corsi, meanwhile, hoisted himself out of the cockpit, pulled his .45 pistol and prepared to duel the approaching adversary from behind the plywood fuselage of the D.III. As the soldier came closer, the Kościuszko pilot noticed the man's familiar four-cornered cap, and taking the calculated risk that he was a Pole, Corsi jerked open his fur-lined flight jacket to expose his Polish officer's uniform underneath. Luckily the rifleman recognized it before he re-aimed his weapon.

Though the immediate danger was over, the Brooklyn native was unable to communicate with the somewhat skeptical soldier. In the meantime, however, a group of villagers attracted by the plane and the shooting gathered around the pair, and Corsi's problem was solved by an Orthodox priest who spoke enough English to serve as an interpreter. As it turned out, the Polish trooper had seen the red nose of the Albatros and assuming that it was a Bolshevik machine, he had opened fire. When the proper explanations were completed, the much relieved pilot was taken to the railroad station where he sent a wire to Tarnopol to indicate his location and to ask for help.

While Corsi lingered quite comfortably for two days with the priest and his family, Lieutenant Chess—hardly thawed out from his own benumbing flight of the 28th—acquired a truck, loaded it with gasoline and oil, and then set out through the penetrating cold to find his lost friend. He and the mechanics with him tried valiantly to coax the cantankerous hard-tired vehicle through the snow drifts on the narrow road. They shoveled, pushed, cursed and regaled, but despite their efforts, the truck finally became inextricably stalled in a fender-high drift. Somehow Chess managed to commandeer a horse-drawn sled from a local peasant, the petroleum supplies were reloaded, and the rescue party proceeded onward to the village where they found Captain Corsi unworried, warm and well fed on potato soup. After a hurried inspection, it was decided that the plane was too frozen up to fly, so it was dismantled for later recovery, and the men bundled up for the chilly sled ride back to Tarnopol.

February was another bad month for the apparently unwanted, seemingly jinxed Kościuszko Squadron. Lieutenants Rayski and Idzikowski were transferred out of the organization, and on the night of the 4th the Lwów Air Park, with its ever-growing store of aviation supplies and parts, was almost totally destroyed by fire. Bolshevik saboteurs were blamed for the conflagration, which also cost Major Fauntleroy's under-equipped unit another plane and a spare engine.

During nine of the next 12 days which followed the destructive blaze, the Kościuszko pilots were again grounded by a stretch of miserable weather, and then, on February 17, the log-book carried several demoralizing notations which seemed to accent the squadron's luckless existence:

> Lieut. Clark attempted to take off. His motor failed and he landed in a pile of dismantled hangars. He was uninjured.
> Lieut. Chess in trying out m.g. hit throttle with his knee, nosing over, breaking prop.
> Lieut. Rorison, trying out heavy prop, hit deep snow, nosed over and broke prop.
> En route to Field, car hit small boy, lacerating scalp.

That same day brought a glimmer of impeding action, though, as Major Fauntleroy, Captain Cooper and Lieutenant Seńkowski left hastily for Tarnopol to be ready to participate in a support mission during a planned offensive maneuver by Polish troops. This was exactly what the squadron had been waiting for, so the men were as excited as school kids with an extra recess. They made it to the outpost city all right, but again fate intervened. A dense fog blanketed the frontline area, and their planes never got off the ground.

That did it!

Cooper and Fauntleroy, originators of the volunteer organization, were so dejected by their lack of combat involvement that they immediately sent a letter by special messenger directly to Marshal Piłsudski at Belvedere Palace. According to Cooper's memoirs, the urgent appeal—which completely circumvented official channels—read:

> The Kościuszko Squadron composed of American aviators has now been serving in the Polish Army over three months. When we came to Poland, we only made one request that we should immediately be sent to the most active sector of the front. Despite this request we are still far away from that position. We now again respectfully request [of] the Chief of Staff that our desire be granted . . . . .

The men were convinced that the special letter achieved its purpose because shortly thereafter the squadron was alerted for shipment. Though the logbook omits mention of preparations for a move, another personal letter penned by Lieutenant Noble—dated March 2, 1920—gave indication of approaching activity:

> I am in Mikulińce now trying to build two hangars, and believe me, it is some job. For tools, I have two monkey wrenches, eight alligator wrenches and some sledges and axes and one drill. The wood for the hangar was picked out of some twenty-eight broken ones that came from the U. S. Army of Occupation at Coblenz, and of

Lt. Harmon Rorison, a fiery little North Carolinian with an excellent World War I combat record, was the first Kościuszko Squadron flyer to attack a Bolshevik force. The event, which took place in the vicinity of Bar, occurred on March 5, 1920, and marked the beginning of the volunteer unit's "shooting participation" in the war.

course nothing lines up as it should. . . . . .My Polish consists of about two cuss words and "good morning," and when the interpreter is away, I have to use German. I sure do have a hell of a time putting my ideas across . . . . I expect the

squadron will fly down here in a few days . . . .
The weather is fine now and the Poles and Bolsheviks are doing a bit of fighting . . . .

Three days later, before the move was made, Lieutenant
Rorison flew a mission of his own out of Tarnopol. He crossed
the Zbrucz River and headed eastward beyond the Podolian
front where he thought he might find some of the elusive
enemy. The squadron log for Friday, March 5—with the
barest minimum of detail—noted that the nervy little Carolinian had observed a "big concentration of Bolshevik troops
and three armored trains at Wolpynee and Bar." What he
did with his machineguns and the bomb or two he carried
undoubtedly will never be verified because the official record
was strangely noncommital and Rorison himself was not
exactly a loquacious man. Two days after the flight, however,
a Polish pilot from the Sixth Eskadra visited at Lewandówka
and reported that "Little Rory" had given the Communists
hell.

It was an isolated incident of a stagnant war, but at last
—at long last—the Bolsheviks had felt the sting and the steel
of the Kościuszko Squadron.

Chapter V

Polish Offensive: Piłsudski's Calculated Risk

It is a characteristic of war that the young men doing the actual fighting are seldom aware of the grand-scale planning of the general staff or the diplomatic strategies of the nation's involved. So it was that in the early spring of 1920, Captain Cooper (age 26) and Major Fauntleroy (age 28) were not privy to the course of action being orchestrated by Marshal Piłsudski. Their desire to get to the front immediately and to challenge the enemy on the field of battle did not necessarily coincide with the realities at a higher level.

The Kościuszko flyers—a bit brash, a bit idealistic and a bit impatient—were dedicated to the Polish cause, but to them the antagonist was Bolshevism with all its attendant evils. On the other hand, Piłsudski, the ex-socialist revolutionary and ardent nationalist, at that time was not particularly concerned about political ideologies or world revolution. His foe —Poland's age-old enemy—was Russia the nation, pure and simple, whether her leaders at the moment were Communists, Tsarists or anarchic freebooters.

The main reason the eager Americans had not been rushed to the firing line was not because they had been overlooked or that their abilities were questioned; it was merely a matter of timing! While Fauntleroy and his men were insisting on action, the Polish Chief of State was engulfed in considerations of immensely greater magnitude. An attempt in January, for instance, to establish an alliance with Estonia, Latvia, Finland and Lithuania as a bulwark against Russia failed primarily because the Lithuanians could not forgive Poland for the earlier occupation of Wilno. Concurrently, the Bolsheviks had launched a time-gaining peace offensive and propaganda campaign among the Polish workers, a move which also appeared to some world observers that Warsaw and not Moscow was responsible for prolonging the international tension. A widespread Bolshevik appeal stated in part: ".... you are deceived when our common enemies say that the Russian Soviet government wishes to impose communism on Poland at the point of the Red Army's bayonets .... At present, the Communists of Russia intend only to protect their own land ... They are not thinking, nor can they think about the forcible imposition of communism on foreign lands"

That innocent-sounding disavowal of aggressive intentions had a lulling effect, but it also generated strikes and unrest among Piłsudski's own people just when he could ill-afford to waste time and manpower on quelling internal strife. Meanwhile, the vacillations and inconsistencies he faced among the Allied powers gave him little solace or strength as the Reds were beginning to overcome the counter-revolutionary forces within their own borders and would soon be able to concentrate specifically on Poland. In February of 1920 the undeclared war was a year old, and on the 12th of that month, the Polish leader indicated quite clearly to a French newspaper correspondent that the relative inactivity was nearing a dramatic end:

> We are left alone to face the eastern problems because Europe does not know what to do. France and England can afford to wait, watch the events and procrastinate. We are immediate neighbors of Russia. We **cannot** wait.

In the United States, Communists and pro-Polish sympathizers countered one another's activities and pronouncements. Secretary of War Newton D. Baker recommended to the ways and means committee of the House of Representatives that surplus military supplies be furnished to Poland— but the wheels of action turned too slowly to be of much help to Piłsudski. On February 28 Major Fauntleroy wrote to Secretary Baker from Lwów to try to get assistance specifically for the Kościuszko Squadron:

> We are operating under conditions almost inconceivable to the average American officer due to the lack of aviation material, and the Poles give us the very best they have . . . . We are not mercenaries. The average salary of one of our pilots is about five dollars a month . . . . If our government could send us twenty or thirty aeroplanes, with spare parts and spare motors we can make good. If this is possible, we need a machine with several hours' flying radius, but would be glad to get anything. If possible we would rather not have De Haviland 4s . . . . Though this may sound like an argument for ourselves, permit me to assure you that the Bolsheviks are the determined enemies of any but a Communist form of Government, and that they will not stop at any method to overthrow the established governments of the world, the government of the United States included. Against the Bolsheviks we Americans feel that we too are fighting for our own country.

Almost a month later Fauntleroy's letter was bucked over to the Secretary of State with the following memo:

> The War Department is not aware of any arrangements which have been made which would justify compliance with the request here made; indeed, without an enabling act of Congress I know of no power in the War Department to

Preparing for a photo session during inactivity while at Lwów. Note that the numbering on the fuselage is also duplicated on the top wing of the aircraft.

furnish such supplies; but as the question of aid to the Polish Army is diplomatic, I take the liberty of referring the letter to you for such advice as the State Department may either now or in the future desire to give.

Apparently the letter was passed on to the Division of Near Eastern Affairs and ultimately filed. At any rate, the

Kościuszko Squadron received no American planes, and no particular encouragement was forthcoming from official sources. In the meantime, on March 11 the unit, with its gear on rail cars, left the station at Lwów enroute to Mikulińce where Lieutenant Noble had been struggling with the erection of a hangar in advance of the unit's arrival. That same day in Warsaw formal talks got underway in a hurried attempt by Piłsudski to achieve an alliance with the Ukraine, then headed by Semen Petlura, whose socialist background and nationalist philosophies were surprisingly parallel to those of the Polish leader. Within Poland there were strong objections to such a pact. It was an empty exercise in wishful thinking, according to some analysts, because the new nation beyond the Zbrucz River was too unstable to live up to the terms of a mutual benefit agreement. Besides that, less than two years before, the Ukrainians had attempted unsuccessfully to wrest Lwów from the Poles, and considerable bad feeling continued to exist because of that particular siege. (It should be recalled, too, that the latter incident was a primary reason why Captain Cooper began thinking of a volunteer force to fight for Poland.)

Despite the divided opinions, however, Marshal Piłsudski persisted in his quest for a partnership with Petlura because he desperately felt the need for at least one active ally for the revived military campaign which he knew was inevitable. Russia's resources—when released from the demands of civil war—were overwhelmingly superior, so all the help Poland could get (regardless of the source) was crucially important to the iron-willed Marshal as his plans for a springtime push approached crystallization. To be successful, he knew he had to strike soon before the Red Army could mass against him, and even as the conference with Ukrainian representatives began, the report of Lieutenant Rorison's encounter with Soviet troop concentrations at Wolpynee and Bar suggested that time already was running out.

Despite the intense urgency, though, the negotiations with Petlura dragged on for six weeks. In the meantime, the

Kościuszko Squadron (little aware of political maneuvers leading up to a major offensive) was getting closer and closer to its avowed desire to meet the enemy head-on. At Mikulińce the flying field was so bad that Captain Kelly—in charge of the train—would not unload the cars until Captain Cooper arrived a day later. He concurred with the decision, and a search for another site was begun immediately while the rest of the men waited impatiently for new orders. The logbook on March 16 featured a succinct expression of attitude:

Still marking time . . . . . Hell!

Unfortunately, there were more aggravations yet to come. Two days later the squadron moved to Berezowica near Tarnopol, and on the 19th, in falling snow, the men began to put up a hangar. On that same date Captain Cooper wrote to Corsi back at Lewandówka:

> I am sending you some food, food for the mechanics, and 160 cigarettes for Clarkie. As I sent your full issue of cigarettes down to Tarnopol, I am not sending you any. Besides this you drew an advance of four boxes when the train left Lwów . . . . I sent a man . . . . to Lwów for a horse and some missing parts of the second hangar. We need those hangar parts immediately and if the man who went to bring them must wait for the horse, I want you to get those parts down to me at once, if you have to bring them yourself . . . . Please pay my hotel bill out of the two thousand marks that Miss Woods [a Red Cross worker] brought from Warsaw and you and Clark may borrow from this two thousand whatever is necessary for your expenses. We are not as well fixed as at Mikulińce but I think we will get along all right.

As it turned out, the hangar parts weren't needed at Berezowica. The very next day—as the snow continued—they took the building down again because orders arrived

Because of the limited range of the planes of that era, bases had to be maintained relatively close to the front lines. Consequently, the squadron's airdrome-on-wheels was an integral part of the operation. Loading and unloading the cars —more than 50 of them including living quarters—was a seemingly endless task.

for them to proceed to the vicinity of Równe where the unit was to be assigned to the Second Group of the Polish Air Force. During the next several days while a landing field was being sought, Lieutenants Noble, Rorison and Seńkowski all turned over in their planes on the rough ground at Równe. Finally, on April 3, Major Fauntleroy accepted a home base for the squadron on the west side of Połonne, a small Ukrainian city of several thousand residents, many of them Jews. The following day was Easter Sunday, but despite the significance of that religious feast to Polish Catholics, the work of setting up an airdrome from which to do battle went on without interruption. A detail of 15 men was sent back to Shepetovka on the old Russian border where the railroad switched from standard European to wide gauge tracks, an old Tsarist strategy to thwart invasion from the west. The crew members transferred the hangar parts and other equipment to rolling stock with appropriate undercarriages, and by Monday afternoon construction work had begun at the field.

An air of excitement prevailed as preparations for some kind of action (not yet defined by instruction from headquarters) proceeded posthaste. At the officers' mess located in the village schoolhouse not far from the field, the pilots discussed the impending campaign—if there truly was to be one—and speculated about its direction and goals. The Polish newspaper, which Lieutenant Konopka translated for his fellow flyers, carried speculative stories of peace-in-the-making, but at the very same time the symptoms of war were all too evident. Meanwhile, the Kościuszko Squadron—alert and anxious—was ready for any eventuality.

During the night of April 9, Lieutenant Weber and an orderly hurried to the thatched-roof house where Fauntleroy and Cooper had found quarters. They brought with them a telegraphic message from the Polish Chief of Aviation which contained the first specific combat orders for the keyed-up flyers: to strafe and bomb a Bolshevik divisional command post and troop concentration at Chudnov, a railroad town some 30 miles east of Połonne. For Fauntleroy, especially, the news of a pinpointed mission made further sleep almost impossible. All the elements of a detailed attack plan raced through his mind as he tossed and turned on the small bed in the peasant cottage. Shortly after dawn the pilots gathered at the schoolhouse to hear the major's instructions, and at precisely 9:40 a.m. a flight of five Albatros D.IIIs took to the air and headed into the morning sun.

The flight was led by Lieutenant Rorison, whose plane carried the squadron's only bomb rack, a makeshift affair alongside the cockpit which held a single missile weighing 12 kilograms (approximately 26½ pounds). Behind him in a stepped-up V formation were Major Fauntleroy, Captain Cooper and Lieutenants Seńkowski and Crawford, all straining their eyes eastward along the railroad tracks in the direction of the target. Although three Kościuszko planes had flown beyond Chudnov as far as Zhitomir on the previous day, the Bolsheviks apparently had not been alerted to a possible air raid, and when the D.IIIs arrived over the Red Army encampment, the surprise was obvious. Bolshevik troopers, horses and wagons scattered in wild confusion as Rorison signalled the attack. Before the enemy recovered sufficiently to retaliate with feeble counter-fire, the five pilots had splattered the area with more than a thousand rounds of ammunition and "Little Rory's" solitary bomb.

From takeoff to landing the flight lasted only 90 minutes, but in that brief time the squadron members who took part got an appetite-whetting taste of what lay ahead. Major Fauntleroy was so pleased with the first sortie that he ordered the planes refueled immediately for a second onslaught shortly after noon. A very disappointed Buck Crawford was left behind when his machineguns jammed, but the repeat attack was as effective as the first—except that the Bolsheviks got off at least 20 bursts of anti-aircraft fire, and even though they caused no particular damage, they gave early warning that future strikes would be challenged from the ground.

That afternoon, as the pilots congratulated one another on the success of their initial organized attack, word was received that several new Italian-made airplanes were awaiting the squadron at Mokotów. Torn by the lure of further combat action and the desperate need for additional equipment, Major Fauntleroy decided that Crawford, Seńkowski, Rorison and Chess should accompany him to Warsaw on the first train they could catch. Captain Cooper was left in command at Połonne, a role he was to fill on numerous occasions in Fauntleroy's absence.

Lieutenants Konopka and Clark (next to the unit's assigned chauffeur) rode in style in the multi-purpose squadron automobile emblazoned with the Polish Eagle. The sedan was used as an ambulance, reconnaissance car, supply transport and pleasure vehicle.

Пропуск в плен.

Важен на 10 дней со дня получения.

Красноармеец! приходи к нам с этим пропуском.
Приноси о собой свое ружье.
Ты получишь хлеб и полное солдатское содержание.
В плену с тобой будут обращаться по братски.

Главный Комисар Центроплена

Kościuszko pilots dropped thousands of propaganda leaflets urging Bolshevik troops to defect. This sheet offered
good treatment and a food ration for any who would come
over to the Polish side. Red Army soldiers wishing to take
advantage of the opportunity were instructed to retain the
paper as proof of their intentions.

During the next several days Cooper sent out numerous
flights on a variety of missions. Chudnov was hit again and so
was Zhitomir. Kościuszko pilots observed and reported a few
scattered cavalry units, all the locomotives and rail cars they
could find, the condition of roads and bridges, and everything
else of value to the Polish high command. In addition, they
dropped thousands of propaganda leaflets on many villages,
towns and Bolshevik bivouacs, an activity the airmen seemed
to resent because results weren't as immediate and as apparent as those achieved by bullets and bombs.

Polish Offensive: Piłsudski's Calculated Risk

In the meantime, the negotiations between the Polish and Ukrainian delegations in Warsaw resulted in a mutual political agreement which was signed on April 21, 1920, not too far from where Major Fauntleroy and his comrades were flight-testing the snub-nosed, heavy-bodied Ansaldo Balilla planes being assigned to the squadron. Three days later a military pact was adopted. The treaty called for joint armed action under Polish command, the provisioning of Polish troops in the Ukraine by Ukrainians, the equipping of Ukrainian soldiers by the Poles, and the eventual withdrawal of Piłsudski's forces when the Bolshevik threat was finally eliminated. On April 25 the Marshal issued a proclamation to the inhabitants of the Ukraine which read in part:

> I want the population of these regions to know that the Polish army entering the territory that belongs to Ukrainian citizens will remain in the Ukraine only as long as it will be necessary to transfer the country's administration to a legitimate Ukrainian government . . . . when the troops of the U k r a i n i a n nation have taken hold of its frontiers to protect their country

The Kościuszko Squadron flew in support of Polish ground troops led by commanders who were unfamiliar with aerial coordination. This infantry unit on parade was accompanied by small boys, a universal custom.

Corsi Collection

The problem of plane shortages was alleviated somewhat with the announcement that the squadron would receive several Ansaldo Balillas (left) to supplement the original Albatros D.IIIs (right).

against new intrusions, when the free nation itself is in a position to decide its destiny, then the Polish soldiers will withdraw . . . . The army of the Polish Republic guarantees to all people of the Ukraine—regardless of class, origin and religion—defense and protection.

Polish Offensive: Piłsudski's Calculated Risk

Before the proclamation was released, Marshal Piłsudski was already at the Polish military command headquarters at Równe, ready to direct the upcoming campaign himself. The die had been cast. On Sunday morning, April 25, a full-scale offensive was launched against the Red Army on a front which extended northward from the Dniester River to the Pripet Marshes. The Kościuszko Squadron—short five pilots and woefully low on gasoline, ammunition and aircraft—was caught right in the middle of the long-awaited battle.

Chapter VI

Bolsheviks on the Run

Captain Cooper, as hard-driving and energetic as he was, spent many ulcerating hours during the two weeks preceding the Polish offensive. He knew something big was developing, and at the same time he was nervously aware of the squadron's deficiencies. The logbook, for instance, began to include a doleful litany of "bad luck" entries, beginning all too appropriately on Tuesday, April 13, with the disturbing notation: "Gasoline and machinegun bullets almost gone."

Wednesday, April 14: No flying due to lack of gasoline . . . . Motor in plane flown by Lieutenant Shrewsbury is condemned.

Thursday, April 15: Lieutenant Konopka shot a hole through his propellor.

Sunday, April 18. Lieutenant Clark crashed up on landing due to hill on field.

Monday, April 19: Flying is called off to give mechanics a much needed rest.

Thursday, April 22: Lieutenant Noble crashes on landing.

Friday, April 23: No flying today due to lack of oil and to orders received to save planes for coming offensive.

When the instructions "to save the planes" came in, Cooper redoubled his efforts to get petroleum supplies which were critical to whatever support mission the Kościuszko Squadron would be called upon to fulfill. He sent Lieutenant Weber in a

Until the squadron returned to Lwów, there was little time for military formalities. The Kościuszko ground crew preferred to work with the unit's planes rather than to march in parades.

light truck to Novograd Volynski, some 30 miles to the north, where a Polish squadron supposedly had some extra oil. The roads (clogged with refugees and military traffic) were impassable, however, and the quest failed. Then he dispatched three enlisted men with a team and wagon, plus another pair of horses trailing behind—to Staro Konstantinov south of Połonne where there was a second possible source of oil. Cooper's orders were crisp and explicit: "Travel night and day. Don't stop to sleep. Take your rest in the wagon. Take turns driving. Kill the horses if you have to. But the oil must be back here in 48 hours!"

Meanwhile, as detachments of cavalry, artillery caissons and infantry platoons churned up the dust on the road alongside the flying field, there were other urgent matters requiring attention. On the day prior to the offensive Lieutenant Shrewsbury made a long reconnaissance flight over the prospective battleground, reporting enemy positions, railroad activity and bridge conditions, all of extreme value to the Polish

95

command. In addition, as he manhandled his Albatros through a heavy windstorm, he located a possible airfield site to which the squadron could move quickly if the advancing ground troops were successful. Concurrently, throughout the day, Cooper and the other pilots studied their orders and the assault plan as it related to air support.

In the portion of the southern sector where the Kościuszko flyers were assigned, the major attack units were the Polish Second and Third Armies under Generals Antoni Listowski and Eduard Śmigły-Rydz, respectively. The former was headquartered at Shepetovka west of Połonne and had as its mission the capture of Berdichev, a grain and cattle marketing center with a preponderant Jewish population. Śmigly-Rydz, a talented 34-year-old Podolian, in turn was assigned two targets from his command post at Novograd Volynski. A strike force of armored cars and motorized transport was to race towards Zhitomir, the principal city of Volhynia noted in pre-war days for its manufacture of kid gloves and tobacco products; while a cavalry division under Gen. Jan Romer was to dash between Zhitomir and Berdichev and make a southerly sweep on Kazatin, a key junction on the railroad leading into Kiev. The Kościuszko Squadron (what was left of it with five pilots in Warsaw testing Balillas and Captain Corsi retrieving his repaired Albatros in Lwów) was to serve both advancing armies with combat and reconnaissance flights as the situation developed.

For Captain Cooper—getting his wish for action at last—the conditions were anything but ideal as the zero hour approached. But there were optimistic notes, too. The trio of enlisted men, dead-tired but jubilant, returned from the south with a wagonload of oil. Another shipment, which included gasoline and ammunition, arrived from a rear echelon supply base. And during the night of the 24th, the flight-inhibiting windstorm lost its sting, after which the Sunday dawn broke sparklingly clear. If nothing else, at least the weather seemed to be cooperating.

A ¾ front view lineup of the Squadron's D.IIIs at Lwów in the winter of 1919.

A quartet of plywood airplanes, meagerly armed and showing obvious signs of age and overuse, received an extra measure of care from Polish mechanics who busied about them in the darkness prior to the jump-off hour. One by one the Austro-Daimler engines were pampered into operation, and promptly at 5:30 a.m., the four pilots—Cooper, Clark, Konopka and Shrewsbury—eased their tiny ships into the air and headed eastward to Mirapol where Second Army troopers were already on the move in the direction of the rising sun. For morale effect the Kościuszko flyers soared directly above the advancing columns and then turned northward to make contact with the motorized attack force along the Zhitomir road. As eager as they were to begin slugging it out with the

97

Bolsheviks, the American airmen couldn't help but be disappointed when the enemy failed to materialize throughout the two-hour flight over a wide portion of the elusive front. As a matter of fact, not a single shot was fired and the pilots had to jettison their bombs in a forested area before returning to the field.

At 9:40 a.m. Captain Cooper and Lieutenant Noble took off again to attempt to find enemy targets ahead of General Listowski's fast-moving units. To their great delight, they spotted a small Bolshevik cavalry patrol which they quickly dispersed and drove into the woods with a diving attack. From that brief encounter they hurried to Berdichev (the Second Army's initial objective) where they emptied their ammunition belts on the railroad station and a small squad of men congregated at a large circus-type tent nearby. Return fire from a Bolo machinegun and several bursts of shrapnel greeted the flyers. Neither plane was damaged, but from that foray on, the air-ground phase of the offensive began to increase in tempo and involvement—and Cooper wished fervently that he had more men and more planes.

A third flight, consisting of Lieutenants Konopka and Clark, almost went for naught when capricious winds caused the Polish pilot to suffer a sudden and intense attack of airsickness. On the return trip, however (despite Konopka's queasiness) the two flyers poured 250 rounds into an enemy armored train at Chudnov. Later in the day Noble and Shrewsbury shot up the rail station at Zhitomir, though Bolshevik defenders were strangely absent. That night the Third Army's motorized advance guard reached the city and captured it without a single enemy-attributed casualty.

Had Piłsudski and his generals planned so well? Were the Bolsheviks reluctant to face a quick showdown confrontation with the Poles, or were the Soviet commanders devising some strategic hide-and-seek ploy not readily apparent to the attackers? It would be revealed later, of course, that Ukrainian uprisings and troop revolts near Kiev and beyond the Dnieper River had thrown the Red forces in the southern sector into a

Bolshevik prisoners were part of the flotsam and jetsam of the Polish-Russian conflict. The squalor of boxcar accommodations—where lice abounded—added typhus and other diseases to the miseries of war.

momentary state of confusion shortly before the offensive was launched. Neither Captain Cooper (as isolated as he was from all the facts) nor the Polish high command, for that matter, were fully aware of the extent of the opposition's internal and counter-revolutionary problems. The fact that Bolshevik resistance on the first day of the drive was virtually negligible generated more quizzical concern than elation among Piłsudski's staff officers.

On Monday, April 26—with Zhitomir already secured—the Kościuszko Squadron was placed under direct orders of the Second Army commander to support the attack on Berdichev. However, its fighting numbers were reduced still further when Lieutenant Shrewsbury was temporarily detached to

The squadron logbook made continuing reference to so-called "pani-wagons" spotted during reconnaissance missions. It became a general term used by the pilots to describe the native horse-drawn road vehicles used by Poles and Russians for supply purposes and by refugees for evacuation.

Novograd Volynski to protect Marshal Piłsudski personally from a possible Russian air raid. Meanwhile, throughout the day Cooper, Konopka, Noble and Clark flew individual sorties ahead of General Listowski's troops, bringing back valuable reconnaissance data and striking hard at Bolshevik units fighting disorganized but aggravating rear-guard actions. On the first of two flights out, Lieutenant Clark attacked machinegun emplacements, a small cavalry force, a troop train and a supply contingent of an estimated 150 wagons. The gutsy Kansan—late of Tulsa, Oklahoma—hopped his ailing Albatros no more than 30 feet above his targets on several diving assaults, and when he returned to Połonne, his plane attested to the enemy's counter measures with nine Bolo bullet holes. The right wing of the D.III was shot up so badly, in fact, that it had to be replaced before the machine could be flown safely again. Clark himself climbed into another plane before noon and repeated his earlier performance on an infantry unit and a wagon train. The second time he managed to escape with only three souvenir holes in his aircraft.

Concurrently, Lieutenant Noble, showing none of the shyness of his first introduction to the squadron, had some aeronautical sport of his own. On a flight over Berdichev he was fired upon by a Red artillery battery and feigning a hit on his ship, he cut his engines and fluttered downward almost directly above the cannoneers who literally danced about their weapon in appreciation of their apparent achievement. Three hundred feet above the emplacement, Noble flicked the Austro-Daimler back into action, trained his twin Schwarzlose guns on the astonished Bolos and sent the survivors scurrying for cover.

Shortly after noon a courier arrived at the Połonne airfield with orders for the squadron to attack the Bolshevik line at Berdichev between 5 and 5:30 p.m., as a softening-up prelude to the final infantry assault on the city. Four weary pilots constituted the "all possible strength" called for in the command instructions, but Cooper accepted the challenge and summoned his men to a briefing session prior to takeoff at 4:30. In his memoirs, he recalled the occasion:

> The Chief of Staff and many of the staff officers had motored out to the field to see us leave the ground. The sun was still shining hot, and I had a violent headache. Some of the dapper staff officers looked at us rather curiously. I was dressed, as usual for flying, in an old greasy pair of trousers, an olive drab flannel army shirt, a pair of dirty, oily puttees and big blunt-toed, down-at-the-heel army shoes. I was bareheaded, as . . . . I dislike anything on my head unless the

weather is very cold. The only thing at all like a conventional aviator in my costume was an old pair of goggles hung around my neck. All of us were tired and under a strain from our many previous flights. It was with relief that I finally received an answering "ready" signal from each of the others as I held up my hand in question to them. I taxied my machine forward, threw open the throttle and rushed down the field which was at last smooth and fine from the work of our civilian population. I was in the air and circled as the others fell in formation behind me. We were off for Berdichev.

The Kościuszko foursome made its low-level strike out of the late afternoon sun, swooping in on the city together before deploying to hit individual targets as they could be found. It was immediately apparent, however, that the Bolsheviks were already evacuating along the railroad to the southeast, evidently hoping to get around Kazatin before General Romer's cavalry could cut off their retreat deeper into the Ukraine. The machinegun squads on the western edge of the town provided a minimal delaying force which the flyers from Połonne quickly drove from their positions. Captain Cooper—with one gun jammed after strafing a cavalry patrol—flew over the city to take stock of the situation. Konopka and Clark turned their attention to the escaping Bolo units which they attacked repeatedly. Meanwhile, Lieutenant Noble spotted an armored train under steam at the railroad station and immediately roared down upon it with guns ablaze. As soldiers and civilians scattered under the onslaught, the train began to move out of the railyard to escape an expected bombing. Machineguns on the rail cars returned the fire of the diving Albatros, and as Noble pulled out of the plunging attack, he felt a sharp, stinging pain in his right arm.

Instinctively, the coolheaded pilot steadied his plane

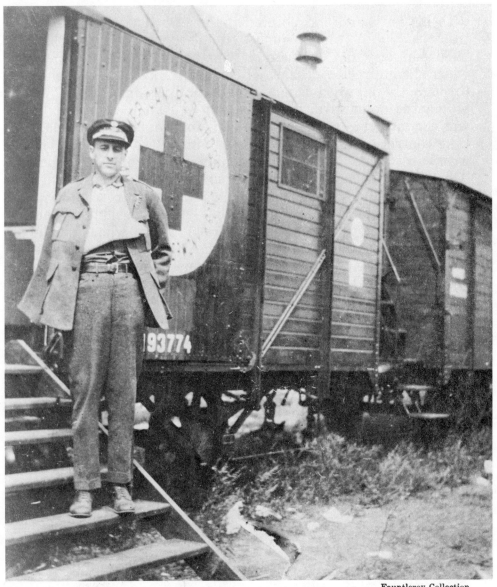

Lt. Edwin L. (Ig) Noble was lost to the squadron permanently when a Russian bullet shattered the elbow of his right arm during a raid on Berdichev. Loss of blood and infection almost cost him his life.

with his left hand and pointed its nose toward the railroad track leading to Połonne almost 60 miles away. A split-nosed bullet—either from the train or from an infantry detachment which had directed a salvo of riflefire at him—smashed through the plywood fuselage and shattered his elbow. As he glanced downward, it was readily evident to him that he was committed to a race with time before loss of blood would take control of the situation from him. Resolutely he flew westward with all the speed he could muster from the riddled Albatros—and somehow he managed to retain his senses until the wheels finally touched down on the squadron airstrip. When the plane came to a stop, however, Noble slumped forward unconsciously over the controls. Those who saw the D.III bounce awkwardly onto the field ran to the ship immediately and eased the crumpled form of the lieutenant out of the blood-soaked cockpit and onto an improvised stretcher made from an old airplane wing. As they rushed him to the nearest aid station, it was obvious to all that the courageous young engineer from Yale made his last flight under the Kościuszko colors.

Lieutenant Noble spent almost a week on a so-called sanitary train before being moved to a Polish medical installation at Kovel where his badly infected wound almost cost him his life. Fortunately, he was transferred to the better equipped American Red Cross hospital at Warsaw in time to receive the care and medication he so desperately needed. Still later he was moved to a larger American hospital in Paris for surgery, and when he was finally able to dictate a letter home, he described the deplorable conditions he had witnessed during his ordeal:

> .... Poland needs ammunition, supplies for the army, real leaders, hospitals, doctors, nurses .... and food. On the sanitary trains the wounded have no food and even no water. The hospitals are hell. The doctors have nothing to work with. Most of the nurses are untrained.

> On the front, shavings and string are used for bandages. In the hospitals they use paper bandages and there is practically no gauze . . . . I owe a great deal to the American Red Cross. If they had not found me, I would surely have gone West . . . .

"Going west" was a war pilot's colloquialism for Death. Happily, "Ig" Noble was spared the premature journey, and for his heroics at Berdichev, he was awarded Poland's highest military honor, the **Virtuti Militari.** It wasn't until he was well on the road to recovery that he learned that in the chaos he had created by his attack on the railyard, a large number of Polish hostages had escaped when their Bolshevik guards ran for cover and the train pulled away without them.

In just two days Polish forces in the southern sector had advanced more than 50 miles and captured all primary objectives with virtually no concerted opposition. That fact was gratifying, of course, but Marshal Piłsudski knew that he must accomplish far more with his offensive than the mere occupation of undefended Ukrainian territory. In simple terms, he wanted to meet and defeat the Soviet force south of the Pripet Marshes before the enemy had time to organize and launch an attack of its own. By winning a notable victory, the Polish leader hoped to establish an independent buffer state in the Ukraine, to convince the Allied Powers (especially an overly skeptical Great Britain) that Poland was a nation capable of directing its own destiny, to convey to the Russian leaders that a western incursion on their part would be met with formidable strength, and to win badly needed support from his own people who were divided by Communist propaganda, torn between political philosophies and—more than anything else—weary and apathetic because of a seemingly endless subjection to the miseries of war.

In their supporting role, the Kościuszko flyers were caught up in the excitment of the advance without particular concern about high command strategies or the political rationale involved in their offensive. They were too engrossed in the hour-by-hour demands of their specialized tasks to worry about Petlura's ability to govern the Ukraine, about the international ramifications of Piłsudski's go-it-alone policies, or even about the fact that they and the Polish troops they accompanied might be moving too far and too fast for their own good. In reality they had little choice but to move with the action, and when Berdichev fell on the night of April 26, Captain Cooper's immediate problem was to establish another airbase within easy flying range of the retreating enemy.

No flying orders were issued for the next day—April 27 —giving the pilots time to recover physically and permitting the mechanics and riggers to make a little headway patching up the deteriorating D.IIIs. At 4 a.m. on the 28th, Captain Cooper, Lieutenant Weber and several enlisted men left by truck to search for a new field location beyond the Teterev River. After a long, dusty ride, they finally found a likely site near Berdichev, but not until they had first been directed to a rough, rocky plot which natives said had been a Bolshevik airfield. The pilots (Ukrainian Communists) had boasted that they would drive all Polish flyers out of the air just as they claimed to have done more than a year earlier at the siege of Lwów. When he saw the place, Cooper realized it was the same spot where he had seen the large white tent which he had raided from the air on the first day of the offensive. At that time the Reds apparently had two of their six planes assembled, but instead of challenging the Kościuszko pilots, they flew back to Kiev and had the remaining four aircraft transported to the rear without removing them from their packing crates. Cooper and Noble (who was with the captain on the particular flight) had won a notable victory over the Bolo air force and didn't even know it.

On Thursday, April 29, Captain Cooper drove back to Połonne to send the planes forward, and on the following afternoon both he and Shrewsbury flew intelligence missions out of the new field. The accurate troop location data they brought back to Second Army staff officers was greatly appreciated by the once skeptical anti-aviation reactionaries who were just beginning to learn how to use their aerial partners.

Chapter VII

The Golden Domes of Kiev

While Captain Cooper and the pilots with him at Połonne were concentrating on the Bolsheviks, Major Fauntleroy and his contingent of flyers were not without their problems in Warsaw. The Italian planes they had received for assembling and testing had some good features and some bad—and overcoming the latter to take advantage of the former proved to be a challenge which would bedevil squadron members throughout the remainder of their enlistment.

The Ansaldo A-1 "Balilla" was a small single-seat biplane, 22 feet 5 inches long with a wing span of 26 feet 1 inch (both top and bottom wings being of equal length with neither dihedral nor stagger in their placement). Powered by an SPA 6A engine of 220 horsepower, the snub-nosed, heavy-fronted fighter was capable of flying 15 to 20 miles an hour faster than the Albatros, could outclimb the Austrian machine by 50 percent and almost doubled the D.III's operating range. At the same time the combination of its heavy engine and short wing span greatly limited the Balilla's maneuverability. This factor had been so noticeable to leading Italian World War I aces that the plane—first introduced in 1917—was never deemed worthy for front-line service. Consequently, only 150 Balillas were constructed, and those which were flown prior to the Armistice were used almost exclusively by home defense units.

Poland's desperate need for aircraft—any kind!—gave the Italians a market for their castoff A-1s, and the Kościuszko Squadron became a dubious beneficiary of the deal. Fauntleroy wasn't necessarily disappointed, though, because he considered the Balilla much better than the Albatros. "They [the Balillas] were like tanks," he said. "You could land them anywhere—and their wings wouldn't fall off." Polish pilots in other units didn't want to fly the Italian planes because of continual engine problems, but Fauntleroy—with the experience gained during his youthful days as a transient mechanic—traced the ailment to low-grade gasoline. To get more complete combustion, he had the jet settings on the carburetors pinched to deliver a finer spray, and thereafter his squadron's Balillas functioned about as well as any planes would have under the circumstances.

When the machines were considered reasonably airworthy, an attempt was made to leave Warsaw on April 23. Stormy weather turned the flyers back, however, and it was during that particular flight that the carburetion deficiencies had been most evident. A week later—after the necessary engine adjustments—they tried again, but Crawford couldn't get his motor started, and Fauntleroy, Chess and Seńkowski had to turn back because of various difficulties. Only Rorison managed to fly as far as Lublin, about a third of the way between the Polish capital and Połonne. On May 1 another flight was scheduled, and this time—after a successful 3½-hour trip from Warsaw to Łuck—a most disconcerting accident occurred. Major Fauntleroy had landed first and apparently left his plane on the open field as he hurried to arrange for refueling. Lieutenant Chess with his vision impaired by the Balilla's conformation, landed directly atop the parked machine, demolishing both aircraft beyond repair. Fortunately, the young pilot escaped without injury; but Fauntleroy's anger was understandable.

(Opposite Page and Above).
Italian-made Ansaldo Balillas were added to the squadron's small fleet of planes in late April of 1920. The snub-nosed, short-winged aircraft were faster than the Albatros D.IIIs and had almost twice as much operating range. The latter characteristic was especially welcomed by the pilots.

(Above and Opposite Page).
After almost three weeks of adjusting and testing the new Balillas, the pilots began the ferrying trip from Warsaw back to the squadron. When they stopped at Łuck to refuel, Lieutenant Chess—his vision apparently obstructed by the plane's conformation—landed on top of Fauntleroy's parked machine. No one was injured, but the badly needed aircraft were reduced to spare parts.

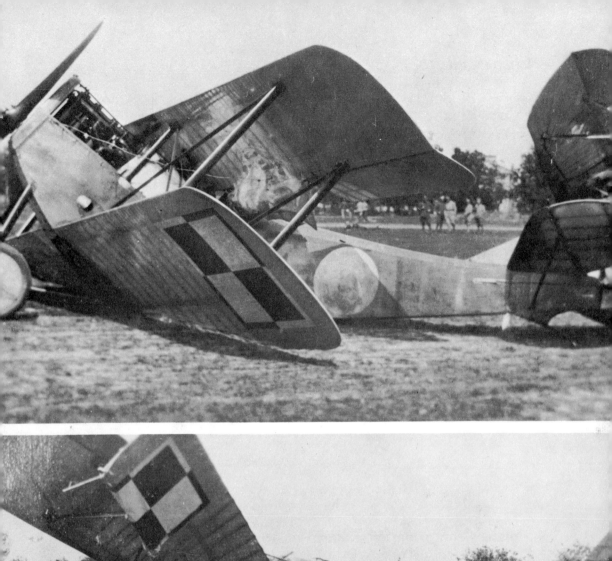

Chapter VII

By Sunday, the second of May, the Kościuszko Squadron was finally back to full strength, although several of the officers were already at the advance field near Berdichev. Major Fauntleroy re-assumed command from Captain Cooper, while the latter turned his attention to preparing the unit's train for movement eastward. At the Połonne base (which was being reluctantly abandoned after a month's stay), pilots, mechanics and riggers gathered admiringly around the new Balillas which, hopefully, would increase the squadron's effectiveness against the fleeing Bolsheviks.

A Polish armored train made an attempt at camouflage using tree foliage. This was used where wide gauge rails were available.

Corsi Collection

The week-old Polish offensive was apparently a smashing success. Resistance was confined largely to rear-guard actions and scattered minor engagements. On April 30 an official communique from Warsaw announced to the world that the forces of Marshal Piłsudski had captured 15,000 Red Army prisoners, 60 cannons, hundreds of machineguns and 70 locomotives as they raced jubilantly toward the golden domes of Kiev, the "Jerusalem of Russia." Kościuszko flyers were sent out, not so much to fight the enemy, but to keep track of the advancing Polish elements. Even before the squadron's rail cars arrived at Berdichev, Lieutenant Shrewsbury was dispatched by truck to Belaya Tserkov, some 30 miles southwest of Kiev and not yet known to be in friendly hands. His mission was to find still another airfield which would permit both the D.IIIs and the new Balillas to range beyond the Ukrainian capital east of the Dnieper River. As it turned out, his assignment grew in urgency as the hours passed. On May 5 the squadron logbook reported: "No flying due to the front having advanced out of range of our aeroplanes."

Shrewsbury entered Belaya Tserkov with the invading Polish infantry, and though hampered by a steady rainfall, he located a suitable airstrip on the outskirts of the small city and immediately relayed the news to Berdichev. During his reconnaissance he learned that Lieutenant Clark's solo attack on the local rail station on May 2 had resulted in the death of six Bolsheviks and one milk cow. Despite continuing rain, Shrewsbury recruited a crew of 50 Jewish laborers to level the field and to prepare the area for the arrival of the entire unit. On Saturday, May 8, Major Fauntleroy flew in, pronounced the location acceptable and then returned to Berdichev to arrange the squadron's forward movement.

Meanwhile, word was received that Kiev had fallen to the Polish Army. On the third of May a small patrol had boarded a streetcar and ridden into the city, actually capturing a surprised Russian officer waiting at a tram stop. The unusual raid was brief and of little consequence, but three

Painting by James B. Deneer

Austrian ALBATROS D.III

Captain Edward Corsi, flying an Albatros, attacked a Bolshevik armoured train. After making several strafing passes, raking it with machinegun fire, he disabled the locomotive, enabling Polish ground forces to capture the train.

The Kościuszko Squadron Emblem

The Kościuszko Squadron emblem was designed by Lieutenant Elliott W. Chess. Thirteen stars and stripes represented the original American Colonies. Superimposed was Tadeusz Kościuszko's red velvet four-cornered cap (rogatywka) and two scimitar-like scythe blades with which peasant patriots under Kościuszko had battled Poland's enemies in the past.

Italian ANSALDO A-I Balillas

Captain Buck Crawford and Lieutenant Aleksander Seń-kowski, in an often repeated maneuver, dived their Balillas on a column of Cossacks. Their machinegun fire inflicted heavy casualties on men and horses and disrupted a Bolshevik advance.

Polowa Odznaka Pilota

The Polowa Odznaka Pilota were the official silver wings awarded to qualified pilots in the Polish Air Force. They were worn above the left breast pocket, suspended from a small chain. The red and white checkerboard was the traditional wing and tail insignia painted on Polish aircraft.

OPIS.

Wzrost _1 m 72 ct._

Oczy _niebieskie_

Włosy _ciemne_

Owal twarzy _podłużny_

Szczególne znamiona

Amerykanin w służbie

_W. P._

Nie mówi po polsku

pieczątka.

K. O. Shrewsbury
podpis właściciela legitymacyi.

podpis wystawiającego
(dowódca).

---

pieczątka.

Ważność legitymacyi na rok _1919_

Lwów, dnia _14. XI_ 19_19_

podpis wystawiającego
(dowódca).

Bezpośrednio przełożone dowództwo:

III-cia GRUPA LOTNICZA

Drukarnia D. O. G. Lwów.

KARTA IDENTYCZNOŚCI.

Imię i nazwisko _Kenneth_

Shrewsbury

stopień _przmerut_

przydział służbowy _7 Eskadra_

Lotnicza (pilot)

rok urodzenia _1899_

religia _protestant._

pieczątka.

podpis wystawiającego
(dowódca).

days later the main Bolshevik force withdrew across the swollen, dirty yellow waters of the Dnieper, and on the seventh the victorious Poles paraded up the uncontested streets. Some soldiers even carried spring flowers in the muzzles of their rifles. It was an easy conquest, a delightful occasion for the troops who experienced the exhilerating march, but a matter of consternation for Marshal Piłsudski and his staff strategists. They knew full well that the enemy had escaped virtually unscathed and that further pursuit—with ever-increasing supply lines and problems of communications—would be a foolhardy undertaking. Historians were to speculate later that the Bolsheviks were the unknowing beneficiaries of their own weaknesses. Some military scholars have suggested that had the Russian forces been better organized, they might have been tempted to make a stand which could very well have given Piłsudski the troop-destroying victory he sought. As it was, the Reds did not choose to fight a major battle, and the Polish offensive rushed to a somewhat empty geographic objective. Unless Semen Petlura could produce—in a matter of a few weeks—the miracle of a united Ukraine capable of discouraging a Bolshevik counter-offensive, then Kiev would almost certainly undergo yet another incursion.

At Belaya Tserkov members of the Kościuszko Squadron were unusually happy and contented in the midst of war. Captain Cooper's memoirs were especially descriptive of the enjoyable conditions in the town of "white churches" on the banks of the Ros River:

Shrewsbury Collection

(Opposite Page).

The identification cards (LEGITYMACYI) of the American pilots were especially important to them during their service in Poland because none of the officers spoke the language of the nation whose uniforms they wore. Lieutenant Shrewsbury's papers were issued by the Third Aviation Group in Lwów.

Fauntleroy and I lived together in the house of a Ukrainian priest, who himself was a charming and courteous gentleman . . . . Just down at the bottom of the hill . . . . Ukrainian girls and boys in their beautiful, many-colored national costumes used to come and sit in the light of the moon and sing their Ukrainian songs . . . . half the night through. But in the day they were still more interesting, for the river would be full of bathers, and in that part of the Ukraine at least, the only ladies' suits were the same as worn by Mother Eve. It was Captain Corsi's favorite delight to rush out to the field in the afternoon, get his aeroplane and come swooping down on the bathers and chase them out of the water and up among the trees on the shores screaming with laughter . . . . in our short stay there nearly every pilot managed to find himself a young and pretty Ukrainian instructor in their language. We danced and sat out at night in the fine spring air and swore undying devotion, and in the morning we were in our aeroplanes far into enemy lines.

Of particular gossip among squadron members was the competition between Corsi and Lieutenant Seńkowski for the affections of a particular black-eyed beauty. Corsi claimed that the Polish officer took unfair advantage because he was able to speak Russian — and, to make matters worse, he got himself slightly wounded in the leg which stimulated the young lady's sympathies and nursing instincts.

Such interludes were a welcome diversion from pursuing Bolsheviks, but the realities of war prevailed despite the comforts and female attractions at Belaya Tserkov. While the occupation of Kiev terminated the Polish offensive in the southern sector, the enemy was not eliminated. As a matter of fact — true to Piłsudski's fears — the advantages of time almost immediately passed over to the opposition. Protected

Polish Medals Awarded To Kościuszko Squadron Officers

Several major decorations were awarded to members of the Kościuszko Squadron for heroism, courage and duty and service to Poland. They are, from left to right: VIRTUTI MILITARI, V Class (awarded to Fauntleroy, Cooper, Crawford, Corsi, Chess, Clark, Noble, Rorison, Shrewsbury and to Rayski, Konopka, Weber and Seńkowski; CROSS OF VALOR (awarded to Fauntleroy, Cooper, Crawford, Corsi, Chess and to Rayski, Konopka, Weber, Idzikowski and Seńkowski); HALLER MEDAL (awarded to all officers of the Squadron); and the CROSS OF THE POLISH SOLDIERS FROM AMERICA (awarded to all American officers of the Squadron).

by the broad expanse of the Dnieper, then almost at flood stage because of the springtime runoff, the Bolsheviks were able to assess the situation, revise their strategies and reinforce their ranks. The Poles, in effect, were stalemated, and the Kościuszko Squadron found itself engaged in the futile effort of thwarting a Red Army buildup.

Not only was the Dnieper River an effective barrier against advances from the west, the formidable stream (third longest in Europe) provided the Bolsheviks with an aquatic avenue for troop and supply movements. Major Fauntleroy's flyers periodically reconnoitered the winding river from Chernobyl south to Cherkasi, observing bridge conditions, steamboat activities, railroad traffic and troop concentrations of any noticeable size. However, just being the eyes of the Polish command would never have satisfied the combative volunteers who came to Poland to fight, not to ogle; so unless their guns were jammed, their ammunition gone or an equally precluding situation prevailed, they attacked what they saw with all the skill and daring they possessed.

On May 10, for instance, Crawford and Seńkowski patrolled southeastward along the river, looking for targets, when the Polish pilot got air-sick and had to turn back. Not wishing to waste the flight entirely, Crawford proceeded alone to Cherkasi where he spotted seven riverboats, three of which were under steam and crowded with troops. Though he carried no bombs, he had incendiary tracer bullets in his ammunition belts with which he knew he could cause considerable damage if he could just get through the heavy counter-fire from positions along the river bank and from the vessels themselves. There was no time for hesitation, however, and giving the tiny Balilla full throttle, he roared into the attack. With both machineguns spewing ribbons of glowing phosphorous, Crawford sprayed his floating targets as he flew an erratic, zig-zag pattern through the retaliatory barrage from below. Three times he ran the steel gauntlet like a broken field runner in his football days at Lehigh. As he pulled back on the stick of his quivering Balilla after the third pass, he glanced back to see a tower of flame leap skyward from one of the boats. Apparently a tracer bullet had found an explosive mark. An involuntary victory grin broke on the lieutenant's lips and he was tempted to loiter long enough to see the final result, but a quick glance at his gas guage convinced him otherwise. (Polish authorities later confirmed the sinking of the transport and told of frightened Bolsheviks leaping into the river to escape the holocaust. In reporting the raid, one obviously embellished newspaper story credited the pilot with dropping a bomb unerringly down the smokestack of the river steamer.) Despite

The Vickers machineguns in the Balillas were enclosed under the cowling, making them inaccessible to the pilots during flight. So when a gun jammed, it could not be repaired by immediate action but had to wait until the plane returned to the base. The same was true of the Schwarzlose guns in the Albatros D.IIIs.

Corsi Collection

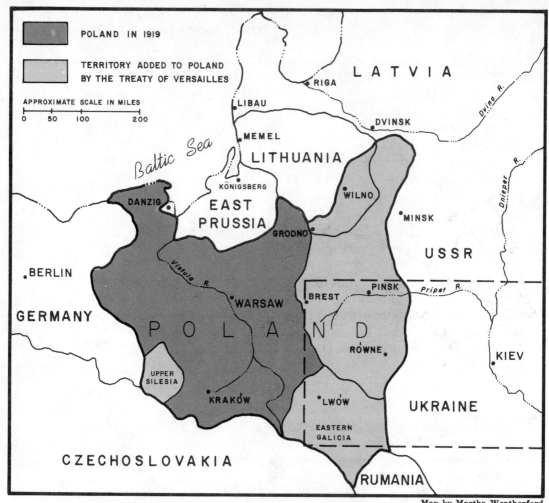

Map by Martha Weatherford

Poland returned to the map of Europe after an absence of almost a century and a quarter as a direct result of World War I. However, disputed border areas became a cartographer's nightmare as international politicians and military leaders failed to agree on permanent boundaries. The Polish-Russian War of 1919-20 was a major, calamitous outcome of the realignment struggle. During its participation in the conflict of age-old enemies, the Kościuszko Squadron operated in the area indicated in the lower right-hand portion of the above map. An enlargement of the unit's combat zone is shown on the facing page.

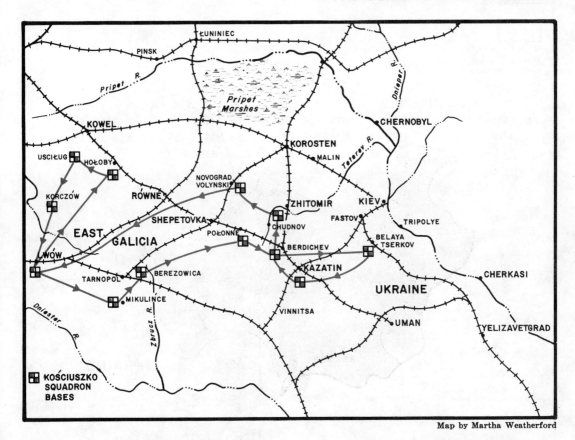

Map by Martha Weatherford

The Kościuszko Squadron's zone ranged from Lwów to Kiev and from the Pripet Marshes to the Dniester River. Its rail-borne ground support moved with the battle action to keep the unit's planes within striking distance of the front. Base locations (marked by the red-and-white checkerboard insignia of the Polish Air Force) were usually pasturelands or other reasonably flat fields alongside the railroad tracks. On some occasions portable hangars were erected, but often the squadron was on the jump again before improvements could be made.

125

The appearance of Red Cross personnel and other visitors from America was always a welcome diversion for the Kościuszko Squadron. The mobile mess hall didn't exactly afford the fanciest accommodations, but company was always welcome.

Corsi Collection

his meager fuel supply, Crawford strafed a Russian train on the homeward trip and then had to make a forced landing near a small village ten minutes by air from Belaya Tserkov. As he climbed from the cockpit, Crawford surveyed the bullet holes in the plane's wings and rudder, shook his head and trudged off to find some gasoline.

The squadron logbook for that date devoted two sentences to the steamboat attack. It was, after all, just part of another day's work!

———

Throughout most of May, the young men of the Kościuszko Squadron enjoyed the kind of existence they undoubtedly had envisioned when they signed the contracts for their Polish adventure. The weather was generally fair. Accommodations at Belaya Tserkov were unusually comfortable. The Ukranian girls were beautiful, and though the enemy had been routed (at least temporarily), there were still endless targets on and beyond the Dnieper which gave the eager pilots all the action they wanted. As a matter of fact, two of the flyers experienced almost more than they had bargained for.

On the 15th, Lieutenant Seńkowski attacked a Bolshevik battery only to have his machineguns malfunction and shoot two bullet holes through his propeller. Fortunately, the weapons then jammed completely, thus preventing total destruction of the blades and an almost certain crash in enemy territory.

Meanwhile, on the same day, Lieutenant Rorison was strafing a detachment of Bolo infantry near the town of Korsun when a lucky shot from the ground pierced his main gas tank. He switched on his reserve supply system, and his engine coughed back into action just before he hit the ground. For some much appreciated reason, the Balilla did not catch fire, and Rorison nursed it along over the treetops for several minutes before he brought it down in a small clearing next to a densely wooded area. Just as the plane bounced to

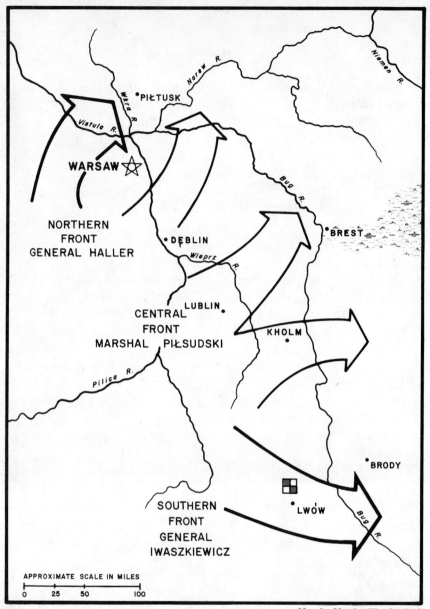

NORTHERN
FRONT
GENERAL HALLER

CENTRAL
FRONT
MARSHAL PIŁSUDSKI

SOUTHERN
FRONT
GENERAL
IWASZKIEWICZ

Naraw R.

Niemen R.

Wkra R.

•PIŁTUSK

Vistula R.

WARSAW ☆

Bug R.

•BREST

•DĘBLIN

Wieprz R.

LUBLIN
•

KHOLM
•

Pilica R.

•BRODY

•LWÓW

Bug R.

APPROXIMATE SCALE IN MILES

0   25   50   100

Map by Martha Weatherford

For the final phase of the Polish-Russian War, Marshal Piłsudski realigned his troops into three fronts. While the historic Battle of Warsaw was being decided by a bold Polish pincer movement, Bolshevik units (including Budenny's Cossacks) along the central and southern sectors were detained and kept out of the capital fight. The Kościuszko Squadron participated in the climatic action from its base at Lwów.

Lieutenant Rorison—known intimately to his fellow officers as "Little Rory"—was the first Kościuszko pilot to strike a blow at enemy forces from the air. His attack on March 5 brought new life to the squadron after a long, frustrating winter.

a halt, he spotted a cluster of people running toward him, and not being able to determine whether they were curious peasants, Bolshevik soldiers or friendly partisans, he jumped from the cockpit and dashed into the forest. To prevent identification in case he were captured, he hid all his Polish papers, his recognizable jacket and his military insignia; later, when night came, he started to walk westward with the aid of a small wrist compass.

After wallowing in a swamp for almost two hours, he finally got back on solid ground and trudged through the darkness for what he estimated to be more than 15 miles. At dawn he came to a small village along a rail line, and to his relief he peered out of the shadows and found Polish cavalrymen occupying the place. Despite aggravating language difficulties (hiding his papers hadn't been such a good idea after all), he finally managed to get aboard a train bound for Belaya Tserkov. Later that night he arrived at the squadron base, tired and bedraggled from a jostling ride in a freight car. He was just in time to learn that all the officers had been invited to a dance organized by the Polish Seventh Division at the town schoolhouse. (Whether or not the tough little North Carolinian had enough energy left for a friendly polka or two was not mentioned in the daily log.)

———

As serious as they were about destroying the enemy, the Kościuszko flyers were not above an occasional practical joke, usually at the expense of one of their fellow pilots. Captain Cooper remembered one such incident quite vividly, because he was the gullible victim of the plot:

I came in late one night from the field, and as I entered the door, I saw everyone grouped around the dining table indulging in a heated conversation.

"What's the big trouble?" I asked, and Shrewsbury pointed excitedly to a huge heap of Bolshevik paper money lying on the table.

"Good Lord, what did you do, rob a Russian bank?" I wanted to know — and then everyone tried to explain all at the same time. I tried to calm them down, and finally the story emerged that a small boy had come up to Lieutenant Chess, handed him a sack, slipped a note to him and then ran away for all he was worth. The message was in Russian, and Lieutenant Weber had just finished translating it.

"To the American pilots of the Kościuszko Squadron: Say nothing! Stop flying! There is more of this to come!"

The note was signed by a ranking Bolshevik leader, and at first I thought sure it was a fake. However, the fact remained that on the table in front of me were almost four million rubles, more money than I'd ever seen before. As I stared at the pile of bills, the argument continued, and then it dawned on me that my comrades were actually coming to an agreement to divide the money but to keep right on flying as though nothing had happened.

By this time I was as excited as anybody, and I shouted: "Are you crazy? If we take this money, sooner or later it will become known, and regardless of what we do, nobody will ever believe that we didn't sell out to the Reds. The whole idea is impossible. It can't be done!"

In spite of my forceful objections, everybody seemed to be against me. I couldn't believe my ears. Here were my friends — as dear as brothers — willing to take a huge bribe from the enemy.

Just then Rorison came in from a late flight, and when he heard the story, he was as shocked as I was. The loud, confused discussion then grew more and more intense, and finally I decided that a squadron mutiny was about to take place, and I started to draw my pistol to end what I thought was a frightening, nightmarish situation.

At that moment Crawford grabbed my arm, and everybody in the room—except Rorison and me — began to howl with laughter. The whole thing had been a well-planned hoax, which almost got out of hand when I went for my sidearm. The money, it seemed, had been taken from a Jewish speculator and propagandist who was

131

under arrest, and while the men were waiting
for a guard from the Polish staff to come and
get it, they decided to have a little fun first.
Weber had written the note, and I fell for it hook,
line and sinker.

From then on, if anybody wanted to get my
goat, all he had to do was produce a Bolshevik
note and say: "Here's another Trotsky for you,
Coop. Better not fly today!"

The Kościuszko pilots continued their periodic sorties
out of Belaya Tserkov, and several of the flyers were ordered to Kiev to operate with a Polish bombardment squadron out of its base near the Ukrainian capital. Though there
was considerable troop activity on the other side of the
Dnieper, the threat of an immediate counter-thrust seemed
remote, and a sense of complacency began to develop as
reconnaissance flights became more and more uneventful
and the excitement of the short-lived offensive faded away.

At 7:15 on the morning of Tuesday, May 25, Buck Crawford took off on a routine look-see mission generally southward from the airfield. His somewhat lazy flight — at an
altitude of little more than 600 feet — took him beyond
Uman and then easterly toward the Dnieper. As usual he
was looking for small detachments of Bolsheviks to attack
and disperse, which was the typical pattern for such forays
into enemy territory. All of a sudden in the distance he
could see the telltale dust clouds which Kościuszko flyers
had learned to recognize as the unmistakable sign of a
cavalry movement — only this time it was different! The
murky billows rose higher than any Crawford had ever seen
before, and as he flew closer to get a better look, he found
himself almost directly above a seemingly endless army of
horsemen resolutely advancing westward over the Ukrainian
flatlands.

There was no question about it. They were Cossacks!
Beneath him was the vanguard of the legendary **Konarmiya**

of General Budenny. Calmly, Crawford tried to estimate their numbers because he knew the information would be absolutely vital to the Polish high command. There were at least six thousand of them, he thought. Then, nosing his Balilla downward, he roared over the serpentine column and emptied his ammunition belts on the startled riders and their fear-stricken mounts. Without pausing to assess the effects of his attack, however, he wheeled his tiny ship in the direction of Belaya Tserkov to give the alarm.

Chapter VIII

Budenny! The Red Army Strikes Back

One effect of the Polish offensive and sudden capture of Kiev was a manipulated change in attitude within Russia which worked to the decided advantage of Lenin and Trotsky. Their efficient propaganda mills translated Piłsudski's actions as an attack — not on the Bolshevik state — but on the "beloved Motherland." A revived nationalistic spirit overshadowed much of the internal division created by the revolution, and the Communist leaders softpedaled their broader international goals in favor of confronting the more immediate problem. On April 29 a general appeal from the Central Committee was not confined — as usual — to workers, peasants and Party faithful; instead, its patriotic entreaty was addressed to royalists and revolutionaries alike:

> Honourable citizens! You cannot allow the bayonets of the Polish lords to determine the will of the Great Russian nation. The Polish lords have shamelessly and repeatedly shown that they care not who rules Russia but only that Russia shall be weak and helpless.

The paradoxical, opportunistic strategem employed by the Bolshevik hierarchy succeeded in arousing broader public support for a "defensive war" against a traditional enemy —

but the most vital factor which would ultimately reverse the flow of battle was little affected by the spirited plea for Russian solidarity. The **Konarmiya** of Gen. Semen Mikhaylovich Budenny, riding relentlessly out of the east, cared very little about political philosophy or its kinship with other Soviet forces. By and large, its members were nomadic, freebooting, illiterate Cossacks who made war for the sake of the war itself. Having completed destruction of General Denikin's counter-revolutionary volunteers, they needed a new enemy, and Poland was the next logical candidate.

Budenny himself was born April 25, 1883, in the heart of the Don River Cossack country. Son of an impoverished peasant, he worked as a farm laborer until 1903 when he served as a private in the Tsar's forces during the Russo-Japanese War. Thereafter he attended the Petersburg Riding School; fought in the Russian Army on the German, Austrian and Turkish fronts during World War I; and when the Bolsheviks came to power after the revolution, he deftly made the switch to the Red banner. Though he did not join the Communist Party until 1919, his ascendancy as a cavalry commander was rapid and unchallenged. British author Norman Davies described him as "a breathtaking horseman who led from the front . . . . the perfect man of action—a prime animal a magnificent, semi-literate son of the steppes."

The First Cavalry Army which Budenny fashioned from wild-riding bandits, partisans and irregulars, became a formidable war machine. Its political commissar was an ambitious revolutionary from neighboring Georgia named Yosif Vissarionovich Dzhugashvili (Joseph Stalin). Budenny, by force of his unusual personality, was able to control the high-spirited Cossacks (from the Turkish word **kazakh** meaning "outlaw"); he knew them well, and he understood what motivated them to fight. Following the victory over Denikin, he gave his lusty followers five weeks for pleasure and plunder. In the United States **The Literary Digest** reported to its readers that the First Cavalry "looked more like a band of robbers than an army. It was dresst (sic) in any kind of garb that could be captured, from the general's cloak with the bright red facings to the simple, torn coat of a private soldier, accompanied, wherever possible, by a piece of Persian carpet as a saddle-cloth." While Budenny waited for new orders, **The Digest** continued, "Wine flowed in streams; pockets were filled to overflowing; fingers were bedecked with stolen rings."

The decision to commit the **Konarmiya** to the Polish campaign was actually made more than six weeks before Piłsudski launched his offensive. The Cossacks were then at Maikop, beyond the Kuban River southeast of the Sea of Azov, more

Counterpart to Budenny's Cossack riders were Polish cavalry units which were an element of the old conventional ground warfare which Marshal Piłsudski and other military leaders understood. Coordinating and utilizing a new aerial force in cooperation with lancers and sabre-swinging horsemen was developed on a learn-as-you-fight basis.

Corsi Collection

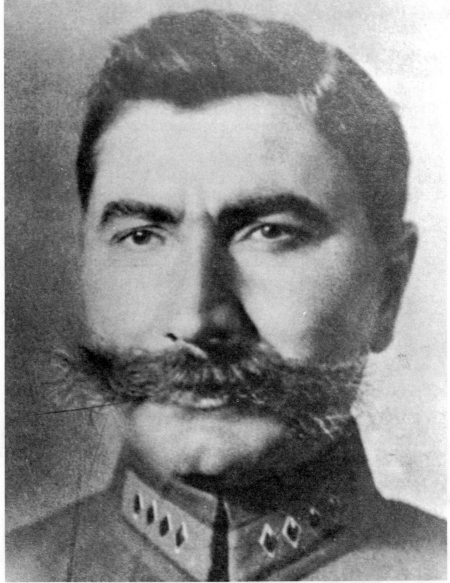

From the Russian Revolution 1917-21 by William Henry Chamberlain, Copyright 1935, Courtesy of MacMillian Publishing, Inc., N. Y., N. Y.

Gen. Semen M. Budenny, the Cossack cavalry leader, was a product of the Imperial Russian Army. However, as the son of a Don River peasant, he was able to make the shift to the Bolshevik cause without difficulty. He died in 1973 at the age of 90, a Communist hero to the end.

than 700 miles from the battleground. On April 3 they began the long overland journey, and on the 25th of the month—when the Polish drive began coincidentally on Budenny's 37th birthday—they were approaching the Dnieper River near Yekaterinoslav in four separate columns. A full month later Lieutenant Crawford of the Kościuszko Squadron spotted just one of the four divisions converging on the city of Uman, ancient caravan stopover of earlier East-West traders, where the **Konarmiya** was to reorganize and prepare for the assault.

These defecting Cossacks were typical of the nomadic, hard-riding troopers of General Budenny's KONARMIYA. They got their historic designation from a Turkish word KAZAKH meaning "outlaw."

Fauntleroy Collection

At Belaya Tserkov the news of Crawford's discovery had an electrifying effect. The Polish command, which was not unaware of the eventual entry of Budenny's cavalry into the war, nevertheless was surprised to learn of its location and movement. The **Konarmiya** posed a threat to the entire Polish campaign. Not only was its strength of numbers capable of brushing aside the thinly scattered occupying units, but its speed and mobility proffered the distinct possibility of a massive breakthrough and encircling maneuver which could cut off the Polish Third Army in Kiev. Under the circumstances it was highly unlikely that Piłsudski's field commanders—with their troops spread across the wide expanse of the Ukrainian front—had time enough to pull together a single force large enough to challenge Budenny in one major, decisive battle. The alternative seemed to be a process of extrication and retreat until conditions prevailed for the Poles to stand and fight with some hope of victory.

As for the Kościuszko Squadron, the sudden turn of events gave it a new mission. Its reconnaissance role was to be intensified because hour-by-hour knowledge of enemy cavalry advances could prevent surprise entrapments of isolated detachments and permit withdrawal to be as orderly as possible. At the same time, stepped-up air-to-ground harassment of Bolshevik units would be a vitally important time-buying factor during a period of great logistical confusion.

Thursday, May 27, marked the beginning of a torturous schedule by Kościuszko flyers in fulfillment of the tactical assignment entrusted to them. At dawn Lieutenant Chess departed on the day's first flight and returned in an hour and a half with 14 bullet holes in his plane. Lieutenant Seńkowski followed him out and returned two hours later with a painful wound in his right thigh and an excited report of a somewhat futile assault on two divisions of Bolo cavalry numbering (in the pilot's estimation) almost 20,000 riders. The third flight was made by Lieutenant Shrewsbury who flew to the Dnieper where he dropped a bomb and fired 250 rounds on an enemy transport. And that was just the beginning.

Unperturbed by his narrow escape earlier in the morning, Chess was ready to fly again on a two-man patrol with Jerzy Weber. They ranged widely over the area where Budenny's columns were advancing slowly but steadily like an unstoppable lava flow. They dropped two bombs on an estimated cavalry force of 8,000 horsemen and then headed for home. Enroute to Belaya Tserkov both planes began to cough and sputter as gas supplies dwindled. The pilots switched over to their emergency tanks, but for some reason Weber's Balilla functioned only momentarily, and then Chess saw the Polish airman go down in a swampy clearing where large rocks were camouflaged by the innocent-appearing underbrush. His own situation was precarious, but the Texan lingered long enough to watch his partner's machine smash against a hidden boulder in a grotesque jumble of splinters and fabric. Chess could see no movement in the cockpit, but thank God there was no fire! With his last ounces of gasoline, he made it back to the field with his report.

Major Fauntleroy immediately sent a rescue party after Weber in the squadron auto, with Chess as the guide. Meanwhile the commander hurried to the Polish staff headquarters with the latest information about the Cossacks. After a brief discussion, the order to abandon Belaya Tserkov was given, and Fauntleroy rushed back to the field to organize the exodus. Where to go was the overriding question, however, and he and Crawford each got into a plane to reconnoiter a possible base at Fastov some 30 miles directly north. On their return, Crawford immediately went back to Fastov by car to get a closer look at a prospective air-strip. In the meantime, Lieutenant Weber—cut and bruised about the head and shoulders—had been lifted from his shattered plane and delivered to the aid station for medical attention.

Throughout the day and the ensuing night, Polish infantry and cavalry passed noisily through Belaya Tserkov as

Squadron mechanics learned as they labored. Unfamiliar with foreign planes (like Lieutenant Rorison's Balilla here), they somehow managed to perform near-miraculous feats keeping the over-worked machines in operation, often on marginal quality gasoline.

the general withdrawal was well underway. Shortly after dawn Lieutenant Weber returned to the squadron, swathed in bandages but ready for work. Fauntleroy assigned the details of packing and moving the equipment to him and Lieutenant Seńkowski, since both were physically incapable of flying duty; and during the course of the day the rail cars were loaded and readied for specific departure orders. A small detail was sent by truck to pick up the usable remnants of Weber's plane, while Rorison flew to Fastov to check with

141

Cooper, Corsi and Clark accompanied Breguet bombers on raids up and down the Dnieper River from their base at Kiev. This plane still had its French markings.

Crawford on the condition of the new field. Then, when he attempted to take off for the return trip, the Balilla's engine refused to start, so he left the plane under guard, and the two pilots drove back to Belaya Tserkov by auto.

The situation was rapidly becoming untenable. On May 29 the squadron train was dispatched to Kazatin, joining the clutter of railroad traffic on the overburdened lines. Because of lack of flatcars, the unit's trucks were sent under their own

Corsi Collection

Captain Corsi was one of three squadron officers detached to Kiev to fly with the Breguet bombers. The New Yorker had a varied military career beginning at 18 when he volunteered as an ambulance driver. He later served in the French Foreign Legion before transferring to the air service.

power with as much equipment as they could carry. Rorison, Fauntleroy and Chess each flew reconnaissance missions, and then all pilots were instructed to fly to Kazatin to share the field there with the Ninth Squadron of the Polish Air Force.

The train arrived at 3:00 a.m. on Sunday morning, the 30th, and some of the supplies were unloaded in the dark by the weary crew. Fauntleroy was in the air by 4:30 a.m., and Shrewsbury followed him ten minutes later in the continuing effort to keep track of the enemy. Later Lieutenant Rorison took off on a three-hour sortie, and when he returned, he was so benumbed by fatigue that he smashed his landing gear as he bounced his plane heavily onto the field. He was almost giddy from lack of rest as he crawled unhurt from the cockpit. Fauntleroy, who was operating on reserve stamina himself, immediately ordered all flyers to lie down somewhere and get some sleep because it was apparent that conditions could very well get worse before they got better.

Nobody objected to the major's command, and soon the Kościuszko pilots were napping gloriously—Budenny be damned! It was a welcome respite, but not long enough. By odd coincidence, a lone Bolshevik plane arrived unexpectedly over Kazatin, dropped its bombs from a high altitude, turned quickly and headed for the Russian rear. The American pilots had waited a long time to tangle with an enemy aircraft, and when the opportunity finally presented itself, nobody could get off the ground fast enough to catch the fleeing foe. Having their sleep disrupted was bad enough; not being able to give chase was even more disturbing. The bombing was ineffective, but the prospects of a sudden breakthrough by Bolo cavalry continued to grow. Before the day was over, the squadron train was reloaded and sent to Berdichev which the unit had left just two weeks earlier on the happier trip eastward.

———

While Fauntleroy was trying to keep the main body of the squadron one jump ahead of the Bolsheviks, the detached flight in Kiev—Cooper, Corsi and Clark—were having the time of their lives flying support missions with Polish Breguet bombers. Cooper's memoirs described a typical attack which took place on May 28:

> . . . . our staff, through its intelligence, received news that Bolshevik land and river forces were about to make a combined offensive against our most southern stronghold, Tripole. We started out from our field at about five in the morning in order to catch the enemy before he could come in contact with our ground troops. We all flew straight to Cherkasi, which was the Bolshevik military port on the river . . . . It was a splendid attack. I saw one great bomb drop directly on a river steamboat, sinking it almost immediately, while one monitor—in its effort to escape the hail of bullets—ran aground. The others all retreated down the river, while we machinegunned and bombed them vigorously.
>
> Once Lieutenant Clark dived so low that it seemed as if he would strike the smokestack of a steamer. That was his specialty, very little maneuvering and a very low attack with machinegun fire . . . . That night our staff picked up a wireless report in which the Bolshevik general commanding in the southern sector said that his attack on Tripole failed due to the disorganization caused by **thirty** Polish aeroplanes. As a matter of fact, there were only eight of us altogether [five Breguets and three fighters].

When they weren't flying, Cooper, Clark and Corsi enjoyed the attractions of ancient, battle-scarred Kiev as if a war did not exist just a few kilometers away. At the Cafe Artistic, their favorite night-time haunt, they listened to tragic tales of life in the Ukrainian capital during the seemingly endless ebb and flow of occupying forces. They laughed, too, with their English-speaking hosts, because none of them were then aware of General Budenny's growing threat to the Polish troops and airmen in the strategic city on the Dnieper.

Chapter IX

A Medal for the Major

The railroad network which interlaced Volhynia, Podolia and Galicia was an important factor to both sides in the Polish-Soviet War. Men, equipment and supplies were shuttled back and forth on the overburdened road beds which had deteriorated seriously during the long years of continuing conflict. Staff officers operated from so-called armored trains —cars sheathed with sheet steel and other protective devices— which gave them more mobility and greater comfort than field tents but which also tied them to pre-determined arteries of movement. The telegraphic system which paralleled the rails was of equal strategic value to Russian and Polish commanders alike. The innovative use of special trains to bring aviation units such as the Kościuszko Squadron within striking distance of a fluctuating front line added to the salience of the railroads. Even General Budenny—in addition to the hundreds of horsedrawn wagons and caissons which accompanied his calvary—had at least four armored trains to serve the **Konarmiya.**

Because of their military worth, the railroads presented a tactical dilemma to the opposing strategists. It became readily obvious that while the destruction of road beds and trestles might impede the enemy on one occasion, it could also rebound disadvantageously to friendly forces which might need the same facilities later to supply advancing troops or to effectuate withdrawal. (Fauntleroy once reminisced about a bridge his pilots had bombed into uselessness, only to learn later that the Poles had been waiting patiently for the Bolsheviks to complete work on the span so it could be used as a river crossing for a Polish advance.) Locomotives became a significant war prize, to be captured rather than destroyed. The same rolling stock—scarce and in poor condition because of overuse and lack of maintenance—was used by Bolos, then Poles, then Bolos again.

Traffic congestion on the lines was unbelievably bad, especially during periods when momentum changed direction and one side or the other attempted quick movements to avoid entrapment. Kościuszko officers soon learned that they had to compete with other Polish units for equipment on various occasions, so commandeering was not infrequent. Lieutenants Weber and Seńkowski—as well as the squadron's native enlisted men—were especially helpful in arranging for rail transportation, even if it had to be accomplished now and then at pistol point. The situation was further complicated along the old Imperial Russian frontier where the rail widths abruptly changed from five feet one-half inch to the European standard guage of four feet eight and one-half inches.

So it was that Major Fauntleroy and his fellow pilots had mixed feelings about trackage, trestles and Bolshevik trains.

They made great bombing targets, to be sure, but they were often of much greater value at a later time if they were undamaged or at least quickly repairable. Yet, when an enemy machinegun on a flatcar sent a fusillade of steel skyward at an Albatros or a Balilla, no attacking airman gave a second thought to the future use of a particular piece of rail equipment when he released a bomb in retaliation.

Railroads were involved in the action at least twice on the last day of May when members of the Kościuszko Squadron flew repeated missions in support of a Polish counterattack southeast of Kazatin. On one of the flights, Lieutenant Shrewsbury was forced down by motor failure some 15 miles east of the field. Because he and the other officers used the track system almost constantly for navigation purposes, the grounded flyer proceeded to the nearest rail line where he located a handcar and physically pumped his way back to Kazatin. He arrived, arm-weary and back-sore, just in time to see a detail of mechanics leaving in the squadron car to find "a Bolshevik plane" which supposedly had come down in Polish-held territory. With no time to rest, Shrewsbury joined the search party and—just as he had suspected—the machine in question was his own worn-out Albatros.

Despite the red-and-white chessboard and Kościuszko markings on the D.III—not to mention his loud protestations in English and through interpreters—he still had trouble convincing the Poles who had found and were guarding the abandoned ship that it was already the property of Poland and

Although Kościuszko ground crew members periodically checked and repacked parachutes for the squadron flyers, Captain Corsi said he never saw a military pilot use one during his entire service in World War I and in Poland. Mostly they were used for seat cushions.

Corsi Collection

didn't need capturing. In time, however, the plane was released by the conscientious ground troops and hauled back to the base where its unsalvageable motor was junked. The incident was then recorded in the squadron logbook as a pointed example of why Polish flyers complained about receiving fire from their own soldiers on the ground; it was obviously a case of continuing mistaken identity resulting from lack of awareness and training regarding aerial support.

Meanwhile, Major Fauntleroy on the third flight of the day in his bullet-punctured Balilla raced southeastward toward the hilly area around Lipovets where a Polish unit of approximately a thousand infantrymen had driven more than twice that many Bolshevik horsemen from a natural stronghold. The major and Lieutenant Chess had dropped their bombs on the harassed enemy during the earlier fly-over, and Chess undoubtedly would have been back for the second effort except that a strong crosswind had flipped his plane upside down when he returned to Kazatin for refueling. Consequently, Fauntleroy went back alone to continue surveillance of the action as it developed and to help with his machineguns and bombs wherever he could.

Apparently the Polish troops were successfully holding the ground they had taken, but as the Kościuszko commander circled widely to the northeast, he discovered an unnerving situation along the railroad between Kazatin and Fastov. A Bolshevik cavalry force—which Fauntleroy estimated at two thousand men—had slipped through Polish lines and was in a position to begin an encircling move on the town where his own squadron was located. When he spotted them from his lofty vantage point, he noted that some of the dismounted men were busily engaged on the road bed itself, and when he looked closer, he could understand the reason for their industry. They were mining the track!

Before Fauntleroy had time to decide whether to attack alone or to go for help, he also sighted the obviously intended victim of the drama. Far in the distance, he could make out the faint traces of smoke from an approaching locomotive, and instantly the major knew what he had to do. He nosed the Balilla around at full throttle in the direction of the train, frighteningly aware that if he could not get the engineer's attention and convince him of the danger ahead, the Bolshevik ambush plan would certainly succeed.

As he got closer, Fauntleroy recognized that the train was a troop carrier, apparently bringing Polish reinforcements to the scene of action south of Kazatin and unknowingly just minutes away from certain disaster. Not only would the mines take a heavy toll as a result of the wreckage, but the Russian cavalry was hidden in the trees on both sides of the track waiting to complete the carnage. Every second was vital, as the major began his signalling with a wing-straining tree-high pass across the front of the steaming locomotive, hoping that someone aboard would recognize the markings on his plane and not construe his maneuvers as an enemy attack. On his second dive, the wildly gesticulating pilot pointed toward the ambush area and tried by facial expression to show the seriousness of his mission. But from the engine cab came a friendly wave and no comprehension at all of the intended message. Again Fauntleroy banked and turned, flying along the entire length of the train trying to communicate with someone by his unusual actions. Smiling soldiers cheered and enjoyed the impromptu, unexpected show as the American airman had to rely on all of his old test pilot skills to avoid the patches of trees along the right-of-way and still stay low enough to have his signals seen.

A terrible sense of frustration mixed with anger engulfed him. He was risking his neck to save their lives, and apparently everyone on the train thought he was some idiotic daredevil buzzing them just for the hell of it. Exactly what happened during the next few seconds Fauntleroy never found out, but suddenly the locomotive and its trailing troop-filled cars came to a brake-squealing, spark-spewing halt. Someone (possibly one of the Polish officers) was curious enough to find out the meaning of the wild aerial exhibition and pulled the emergency cord.

By another stroke of luck, the train stopped near a small clearing, and Fauntleroy was able to land his Balilla in full view of his beneficiaries. He vaulted from the cockpit and raced toward the officers emerging from the cars. In his oil-spattered flying gear he knew he would have difficulty identifying himself, but as he ran, he clawed at an inside pocket to find his official papers—his **Legitymacyi.** "Can anyone speak English?" he shouted, as he approached the understandably puzzled Poles who were still not sure of his purpose. To his great relief, a young lieutenant stepped forward, hurriedly checked the pilot's credentials, and then—in a torrent of words in two languages—the ominous reason for Fauntleroys's acrobatics became clear to everyone.

There was a quick but sincere show of appreciation, and —after a hasty consultation—the Polish troop commander ordered the soldiers from the train and into tactical formation on each side of the track. As the infantrymen began to move forward to ambush the ambushers, Fauntleroy returned to his plane, managed a successful takeoff from the confined, tree-rimmed field and prepared to add his firepower to the attack. In the ensuing skirmish, the Bolsheviks—their plan gone awry—were as much the victims of their own confusion as they were of the surprise assault by the forewarned Poles. Fauntleroy himself dropped his two bombs and ripped into scattered bands of Bolos with 400 rounds from his twin machineguns. Then, with his ammunition gone and his gas supply ebbing, he pointed the Balilla homeward toward Kazatin. He had, after all, put in a full day's work!

———

The major's courageous act did not go unrecognized. Before he returned to the United States months later, he was to

Marshal Piłsudski himself decorated Major Fauntleroy with the VIRTUTI MILITARI, Poland's highest award for valor.

receive Poland's highest decoration for valor—the **Virtuti Militari**—and one of the heroic achievements which earned him the cherished medal was his role in the dramatic railroad episode which took place on his own nation's Memorial Day, 1920.

Chapter IX

Despite the efforts of the Kościuszko Squadron—however valorous—the tide of the war had definitely changed. Ascertaining the enemy's strategy while trying desperately to avoid the disintegration of withdrawing armies kept Marshal Piłsudski's generals glued to their field maps, attempting constantly to piece together bits of information on Bolshevik movements and scattered rearguard engagements so that intelligent decisions could be made. In the meantime, small unit commanders like Major Fauntleroy had to be prepared to operate independently should a general collapse occur.

Southeast of Kazatin, outnumbered Polish troops stubbornly pressed their attack on enemy cavalry forces with the help of Kościuszko planes, but by the fifth of June (when rain and heavy fog curtailed the effectiveness of aerial support), the increased concentration of Bolshevik columns pushing forward across the entire irregular battleline posed a massive threat, not just to the units directly involved, but to the future of Poland.

From Kiev Captain Cooper had sent a message to Fauntleroy asking for more flyers in the capital city. Lieutenant Clark—worn down from overwork and lack of sleep—had been evacuated with a serious case of pneumonia which, as it turned out, was to remove him permanently from the squadron's roster. Cooper wanted a replacement for the fearless Kansan—plus others—to continue the escort mission with the Breguet bombers against the Bolo flotillas on the Dnieper. However, because of Fauntleroy's knowledge of developments elsewhere (especially the relentless advance of Budenny's tireless Cossacks), he rejected the captain's request and instead ordered Cooper and Corsi to rejoin the squadron immediately at Kazatin. The showdown was at hand, and the Kościuszko commander wanted to be as well prepared for it as possible under the foreboding circumstances.

Chapter X

The Long Road Back

On Sunday, June 6, the daily report in the Kościuszko Squadron's logbook began with a brief negative note: "This day scheduled for a Polish offensive but the Bolos beat [us] to it in the night."

Actually, the single-sentence summary referred—not to a mere localized drive as it may have sounded—but to a major Russian campaign designed to sweep the forces of Marshal Piłsudski out of the Ukraine and all the way back to Warsaw. The Red Army's offensive started officially on May 26, but Polish resistance had blunted the initial thrusts, aided and abetted by such air units as the Kościuszko Squadron and the Breguet bombers flying out of Kiev. During the afternoon of June 5, however, the heavy pressures of superior numbers finally prevailed, and the anticipated general breakthrough became a reality. Bolshevik troops, having crossed the Dnieper north of Kiev, swung southwestward to span the Kiev-Korosten railroad. From the southeast General Budenny's Cossack divisions drove northwesterly toward Belaya Tserkov and Kazatin, forming the bottom half of the pincers intended to cut off the Ukrainian capital. (The Russian successes had an effervescent effect on Bolshevik morale, and for three decades afterwards the Red Army celebrated June 5 to commemorate "the first victory of the Soviet military art over European arms.")

The day after the Bolo surge, pilots of the Kościuszko Squadron were in the air from dawn till dark. The logbook recorded a continuing schedule of one-man missions:

> **1st Flight:** Captain Cooper follows railroad line southeast of Kazatin .... locates our troops and ten thousand Bolsheviks advancing on Ruzhin .... He attacks them with two bombs and 200 rounds of ammunition.

The Poles used tanks like the one above in defense of Kazatin, but the mobility of Budenny's cavalry and his strength of numbers overcame all major resistance. The retreat became a delaying action in which the Kościuszko Squadron figured prominently.

Corsi Collection

2nd Flight: Captain Corsi goes to Ruzhin and observes . . . . 700 enemy cavalry. Dropped one bomb on them. Perfect hit observed. From Ruzhin to Bielowka observed 300 enemy cavalry and 50 wagons; drops second bomb and fires 100 rounds.

3rd Flight: Lieutenant Chess goes to Bielowka and Ruzhin . . . . Notices bridge blown up on railroad line near Bielowka and 250 enemy troops . . . . Dropped two bombs and fires 150 rounds.

4th Flight: Lieutentant Rorison . . . . locates our troops and tanks guarding Kazatin . . . . enemy advancing north from Ruzhin in large numbers. Fires 500 rounds . . . . altogether he observes eight columns of enemy cavalry of about 12,000 in all.

5th Flight: Captain Corsi goes to Bielowka and Ruzhin and observes that cavalry had turned northeast to cut railroad to Fastov. Fires 100 rounds, dropped two bombs.

6th Flight: Lieutenant Chess goes to Ruzhin . . . . to southern railroad line and back to Berdichev. Observes road bridge blown up; fires 200 rounds; drops two bombs on enemy cavalry.

7th Flight: Captain Cooper goes on reconnaissance but has forced landing due to motor trouble five kilometers east of Kazatin. Returns to Kazatin and secures truck and mechanics who repair motor. He takes off again and makes a reconnaissance along Fastov railroad line and observes enemy patrols in forest northeast of railroad track and Kazatin. Returns to Berdichev.

8th Flight: Captain Corsi flies in heavy rain storm and intense fog from Berdichev to Bialopole to railroad and there observes patrols around railroad. [He then reconnoiters in the] vicinity northeast of Berdichev and finds no enemy.

(Above and opposite page).
During the retreat from Belaya Tserkov, the squadron train was moved many times and often at short notice. Though it was against regulations, refugees took advantage of extra space on the flat cars to flee westward. The distinctive radiator identifies the large truck in the upper picture as an American Packard.

During the hectic day, the squadron operated out of both Kazatin and Berdichev, hardly more than 20 miles apart. Major Fauntleroy had intended to participate in the patrols but his Albatros burned up on the latter field as he was trying to take off. He then boarded a train for Kazatin where he picked up Lieutenant Seńkowski's Balilla and flew it back to Berdichev. Lietutenant Shrewsbury, meanwhile, had to sit out the action because his guns wouldn't function.

With the enemy pressing forward so rapidly, the possibility of the squadron train being captured by a sudden burst through the lines grew with every hour. Major Fauntleroy sent the unit to Berdichev and then on to Zhitomir early in the morning of June 7. Before the day was over, however, it became apparent that Budenny's horsemen had the momentum to endanger all Polish positions east of the Słucz River, so the ground crew was alerted for still another impromptu move. While the other flyers tried to get a hurried nap, Fauntleroy himself flew a reconnaissance mission during which he recognized almost immediately that Zhitomir could not possibly be held. His subsequent actions were vividly described in Merian Cooper's unpublished memoirs:

During the general retreat, every effort was made to prevent aviation materiel from falling into Bolshevik hands. On several occasions non-functioning planes—like this Balilla—were burned ahead of the advancing enemy.

He banked his aeroplane far over, executed a lightning turn, opened his throttle as far as it would go, put the nose of his ship down below the line of the horizon in order to gather more speed and was off like a flash of a gun to give the alarm. He flew straight over our transport, firing a burst of bullets as he went, our signal that the enemy was almost on top of us. It was an order .... to evacuate immediately. As he flew to the field a kilometer farther on, Lieutenant Weber, who had been awake, was already directing the evacuation. The pilots were hastily pulling on their clothes and rushing to the field . . . . Fauntleroy landed, jumped from his aeroplane the second it had come to a stop and ran for all he was worth to the nearest automobile a half a mile away. He jumped to the wheel himself and driving the car as fast as it could go, sped to staff headquarters. The staff acted instantaneously. Valuable papers and maps were swiftly carried aboard the cars; our transport was switched on behind the staff locomotive . . . . [and] as the train steamed west to Novograd Volynski . . . . Budenny's cavalry came riding into town from the other side.

The long road back had begun, and somehow the gravity of the situation was accentuated by the string of misfortunes which followed in the squadron log:

Captain Cooper, Lieutenants Weber, Chess and Shrewsbury start on raid with bombs south of Kazatin. Captain Cooper's engine quits on takeoff and being unable to start motor, [he] later burns his plane. One of the bombs on Lieutenant Shrewsbury's plane comes off on the takeoff and crashes through his right horizontal stabilizer and elevator. He, observing this in the air, goes to Zhitomir and lands. Lieutenants Weber and Chess go to Kazatin but are prevented by ground fog from finding the enemy, and return to Zhitomir, having dropped bombs on vacant field.

Lieutenant Crawford tried to take off in Balilla but motor does not turn up and he flies four kilometers at 100 meters, when machine catches on fire, and he lands and fires a few shots in his gas tank to help along the fire. He then walks northwest to Piatkl, 30 kilometers, where he

joins retreating Polish transport to Połonne and
then Shepetovka .... Captain Cooper .... goes
in Opel car in search of Lieutenant Crawford
He does not find him but succeeds in finding two
mechanics who had [also] gone in search of him.
They then get stuck in the mud and are forced to
abandon the car. They walk 20 kilometers and secure a train to Shepetovka.

At Novograd Volynski all squadron members who had
finally arrived there worked through the night on the dimin-
ishing fleet of planes which had been moved into an old shed
for temporary protection. What they did not know at the
time was that shortly after they had evacuated Zhitomir,
Budenny's Fourth Division smashed into the town, routed
the remaining Polish defenders and released some 5,000 Russian prisoners. Almost simultaneously the **Konarmiya's** 11th
Division engulfed Berdichev, and shortly afterwards the
gruesome word filtered out that the hospital there—with 600
wounded Poles apparently entrapped—had been burned to
the ground.

On the morning of June 8 wind and rain made flying almost impossible, but the doughty Rorison still attempted a
sortie in the direction of Berdichev. His Balilla simply
couldn't cope with the elements, however, and after being
blown off course by the storm, he landed on the Ninth Squadron's field at Połonne. After refueling, he tried again, with
even less success. While he hedgehopped over a swampy area,
his engine coughed and quit, and with no gliding altitude to permit him even a momentary choice of a landing
site, his plane splashed down into the marsh and Rorison
was catapulted out of the cockpit as the Balilla flipped over
into the morass. How long he lay unconscious near the wreckage was not included in his report, but when the delayed two-
sentence entry of his escapade was finally recorded in the
sqadron log, it said merely that he woke up "as a Russian
peasant [tried] to force muddy water down his throat." The

groggy but resilient lieutenant didn't waste any time in the swamp, because shortly afterwards he made his way back to Połonne where he caught a train to rejoin his unit.

In the meantime, Lieutenant Shrewsbury was ordered up into the inclement weather to carry special orders from the Polish General Staff to the Third Army in Kiev whose situation was growing more and more precarious. While Shrewsbury was enroute, a second set of orders—reputedly countermanding the first—was entrusted to Lieutenant Weber for urgent delivery. The Bolshevik pincers were gradually closing in on the escape route for the troops of Śmigły-Rydz, and the planes of the Kościuszko Squadron provided a vital communications link in the critical hours during which the future course of the war was directly affected. With the Poles in retreat all across the southern sector, entrapment and destruction of an entire army command—the Third—might well have given the Bolsheviks a decisive victory of such proportions that Piłsudski's hard-pressed and scattered forces could never have recovered.

But the smashing blow never came!

On June 9 Major Fauntleroy flew a reconnaissance mission over the Zhitomir area and reported that Budenny's troops there had circled back toward the east apparently as part of the strategy to seal off Kiev. On the 10th Fauntleroy refused to order any of his pilots into the air because of the rain, fog and heavy winds which blanketed the region. As it turned out, his decision was sustained when the planes from the Polish Fifth Group staggered into Novograd Volynski with the news that the evacuation of Kiev was underway. The airfield there had been abandoned; gasoline stores had been destroyed; and the mechanics had already left with the ground troops.

––––––

At the particular time, it was not possible to assess how or why certain events occurred. The annals of warfare are replete with examples of lost opportunities, command quirks

Accommodations at Lewandówka field at Lwów were not pretentious, but they were better than the other bases used by the squadron during the offensive and the retreat. Mechanics were working on Albatros D.IIIs when this picture was taken.

and wrong decisions, and Semen Budenny—for all his military skills—proved that he, too, was not infallible. Though historians continue to argue the point, the fact remains that the Bolshevik forces which charged into Zhitomir and Berdichev with such potency did not immediately pursue their advantage over the reeling Poles, nor did they proceed northward to complete the encirclement of the Third Army. Instead, a brief lull occurred in the action following the Russian victories on June 7, and then Budenny ordered his Cossacks in the center to double back and cut off the Kiev-Kazatin railroad on which he assumed the corraled enemy would attempt to escape. What happened, of course, was that Śmigły-Rydz sent his command northwesterly along the Kiev-Korosten line to which the Bolsheviks had given secondary attention, and this momentary lapse on the part of the Russians provided time enough for their intended victims to withdraw in the direction of Warsaw where their presence in the weeks to follow would prove of incalculable value.

Meanwhile, the Kościuszko Squadron—its members approaching physical exhaustion, its supplies depleted and its small fleet of planes almost eliminated—was ordered back to Lwów to refit and recuperate for the impending last stand.

However, on June 12—just before the unit was relieved from its frontline duty—two more planes were put out of commission. When Konopka and Corsi attacked a Bolshevik cavalry detachment, the latter's ship was hit five times by concentrated ground fire. Two longerons were shattered, and fearing collapse of his weakened fuselage, the New Yorker immediately headed for the base at Novograd Volynski. Recognizing that his partner was in trouble, Konopka flew as closely as possible to the crippled craft so that he was readily available for whatever assistance he could give. About a mile from their destination, Corsi signalled that he couldn't make it, and together they eased down—side by side—on a small field. The damaged machine buckled instantly when the tail hit the ground; and to compound the destruction, the Polish pilot was so intent on watching how Corsi was faring that he failed to see a sizeable tree loom up ahead of his own plane. The second crash was worse than the first, but fortunately the two flyers escaped with no more than bruises. Obviously, it was time for a respite!

————

After avoiding disaster on the banks of the Dnieper, the Polish ground forces in the southern sector managed to reestablish their lines sufficiently enough so that the rearguard resistance had at least a modicum of cohesion. For their part, the Bolsheviks dallied instead of capitalizing on the offensive momentum, and the brief hesitation provided the Poles with the breathing spell they so desperately needed.

Major Fauntleroy and his pilots were ready for a breathing spell, too, but before the entire squadron could regroup in Lwów, Captain Corsi and Lieutenant Weber were temporarily assigned to Gen. Jan Romer, the Polish cavalry commander, who needed them for reconnaissance purposes. For a week—when they weren't weathered in—they flew from an undeveloped field near Shepetovka where they and four mechanics with them virtually lived off the land. Logbook notations gave evidence of a particular ration problem:

Shrewsbury Collection

Portable Bessonneau hangars, developed by the French for World War I, were used by the Kościuszko Squadron on isolated bases where no other shelter was available for the unit's planes. A wood-and-canvas Bessonneau is shown as a completed structure (above) and in the erection stage (below).

Corsi Collection

June 14: The field is very good but too small. No food in the village but plenty of strawberries in the woods.

June 15: No flying. Rain. No food—strawberries.

June 16: No flying. Un peu food—too many strawberries.

The remainder of the detached service was relatively uneventful, and by the 23rd of the month, the squadron in its entirety was back at Lewandówka field where eight months earlier the Americans had first joined the unit. New Balillas were delivered to them there for testing and familiarization flights—but, more than anything, it was time to rest and revitalize, and the young officers took full advantage of the opportunity.

Back in the United States the Polish-Russian war received ho-hum treatment in the press during the month of June when Marshal Piłsudski's dream was almost crushed and the Kościuszko Squadron virtually reduced to an exhausted, planeless ground unit. Belatedly, however, the War Department began to show at least a glimmer of interest in what the American flyers were doing in the far-away Ukraine, and a classified report of their activities was solicited for possible use by the American Air Service in future operations. The official document read, in part:

During the retreat of the Polish Army from Kiev . . . . aviation was used probably for the first time in the rear guard of an army. Previously the use of aviation for this purpose was considered impractical due to the great technical difficulties in constructing suitable flying fields and the danger of capture of all aviation material . . . . as it usually takes several days to properly pack and load the equipment of a squadron for transfer from one field to another.

The fields used were located from 5 to 50 kilometers from the front. Frequent moving was necessary. There was neither time nor personnel to prepare the fields . . . . No small tents were available. Bessonneaus were erected when possible but some fields were used without any shelter for the planes. It was found important to keep the squadron very mobile. Everything possible was left on the railway trains. Personnel were quartered there. Fifty-seven cars were required for the squadron. For changing fields the railway was used almost exclusively. Only five auto trucks were available, and those were in bad condition. There was one touring car. Consequently, the fields had to be near the railway lines.

The availability of flying fields was of continuing concern to aviation unit commanders in Poland and the Ukraine. Accessibility to a railroad siding was of prime importance, and occasionally it was necessary to remove the humps and bumps of pastures and croplands to make acceptable landing strips.

Corsi Collection

When the Bolshevik cavalry approached too near a field, everything except the planes, a few mechanics and the serviceable trucks were shipped by train to a previously selected field in the rear . . . . In 10 days the squadron moved its field five times . . . . There was no opposition from Bolshevik aviation . . . . The outstanding feature of this operation was the rapid advance and effectiveness of Bodena's [sic] mounted army. This force consisted of four cavalry divisions of three brigades each with a total of possibly 20,000 men . . . . This force was extremely mobile and covered remarkable distances. In one day they would march 70 kilometers and do the same the following day. They habitually advanced along river beds and on forest trails, always avoiding the main roads . . . . The aviation was able to follow them with the greatest ease except during the very early morning or late at night when they camped in heavy forests. The habitual method of march was in columns of threes unless the route rendered this impractical. The columns were often 15 kilometers long and were kept closed up. Wagon trains followed in the rear of the columns . . . . at the rear of each squadron was a light two-wheeled horse-drawn cart with a machinegun mounted on it. Advance guards were small in number and only two or three kilometers ahead. Flank patrols were numerous and from 15 to 20 kilometers from the column. A small amount of light artillery accompanied the columns, as well as a number of armoured cars.

During this operation the [Kościuszko] Squadron had eight pilots and 14 single place scout aeroplanes . . . . After locating the column the pilot would fly well out of range to a point about one half mile behind the rear of the column and then at a height of about 300 meters would fly

Field repair was generally accomplished by hand labor. Destitute Jewish victims of the war were often employed for such menial tasks.

back over . . . . the wagon trains and the rear of the cavalry [where] the two bombs would be dropped. After dropping the second bomb, the pilot would dive upon the troops and at a height of 100 meters open fire with both machineguns . . . . At this period of the attack the wagon trains and the rear of the cavalry would commence scattering in all directions, and with the number of killed and wounded men and horses, the confusion is very great. The pilot . . . . would open his motor full so that the roar would have a frightening effect on the horses. Flying directly down the line by elevating and lowering the nose of the plane a very slight degree while at a height of 10 to 15 meters above the column, machinegun bullets could be sprayed through the entire length of the column, this causing casualties and creating great disorder and confusion. By this method one squadron was able to check the advance of 20,000 cavalry for several hours every day . . . . For this sort of warfare scout pilots of considerable skill are necessary as they must land on unimproved fields and must be capable of maneuvering their planes rapidly at extremely low altitudes.

To meet these aeroplane attacks, the Bolsheviks placed machineguns on wagons at the head and rear of the columns but with little success as the horses became frightened and unmanageable after the bombs were dropped . . . . A more effective method was—upon the approach of the plane—to have different units throughout the column dismount and hold their horses by the reins. The dismounted men could deliver a more effective fire and better control their horses.

This description of the use of aviation on the Bolshevik front was obtained from American aviators in the Kościuszko Squadron. The statements are endorsed by all of the officers of this unit and can be considered very reliable . . . . The value of these operations lies in the fact that the warfare on the Polish-Bolshevik front is similar to that which would be encountered in Mexico . . . . The squadron recommends that the American Air Service devise some sight for bombing from single-seated scout planes. These sights should be simple and be constructed for use at fixed altitude . . . . The work of this squadron on the Bolshevik front has been extremely commendable and has been highly praised by the Polish High Commanders.

Indeed, the exploits of Major Fauntleroy and his cohorts were meritorious and consequential to the continued existence of Poland. They had—as the War Department report indicated—delayed the advance of Bolshevik cavalry long enough for the Polish infantry to withdraw in orderly fashion and to strengthen its strategic positions. Budenny was still on

the offensive in the Ukrainian sector, however, and the Kościuszko flyers made the most of their interlude in Lwów because they knew they would be back on the battleline in a matter of a few short days. The Cossacks, they feared, might even
speed up the timetable.

Chapter XI

The Time of Reckoning Has Come

While the Kościuszko pilots sojourned in Lwów, the fortunes of war continued to favor the attacking Bolsheviks as the Poles were driven back begrudgingly on all fronts by an exuberant enemy. Coincidentally, on the Fourth of July—as the American flyers were being feted at a public Independence Day commemoration at the Lwów city hall—the Red Army launched its grand offensive in the northern sector to crush the Polish Eagle in its most prominent aerie: the capital city of Warsaw. Mikhail Nikolayevich Tukhachevsky, the 27-year-old commander-in-chief of the assaulting force, issued a poetic, morale-inspiring general order: "Soldiers of the Red Army! The time of reckoning has come . . . . Over the dead body of White Poland shines the road to world-wide conflagration. On our bayonets we shall bring happiness and peace to toiling humanity . . . . On to Vilna, Minsk and Warsaw! March!"

It was a time of reckoning for Marshal Piłsudski, too, as his plan for a strong, proud Poland faced its greatest (and possibly its final) challenge. The Western Powers — so diplomatically entangled that historians may never figure out completely who did what to whom — hampered more than helped the Polish cause. Labor leaders and socialists around the world demanded a "hands off Russia" policy; and within Poland, Communist agitators did everything they could to

(Above, left and opposite page)

Throughout Poland women responded to the national emergency. Many of them were equipped and trained in combat arms to augment male forces in the defense against the Red Army invasion.

Polish women's battalions, which had performed so heroically in the first siege of Lwów by the Ukrainians, were mobilized again to help ward off the Bolshevik invasion in 1920.

generate the revolution which Lenin so confidently assumed would erupt with the invasion. It was a time of grave anxiety, but Piłsudski — in the words of English poet William Cowper — had the seemingly innate ability "to seize with power the crisis of a dark decisive hour."

On July 8 the Associated Press datelined a story from Warsaw which emphasized the intensity of preparations for a last-ditch stand:

The Bolshevik high command entrusted the capture of Warsaw to 27-year-old Mikhail Tukhachevsky. Brilliant though he was, the young general was defeated by the Polish defenders when Budenny's Cossacks failed to arrive from the Galician front.

Volunteers for immediate service against the Bolsheviki are called for by the Polish National Council of Defense in a manifesto issued today. Those unfit for active service are urged to register that they may be called on to relieve able office men. The document is signed by President Piłsudski and says that the war is against the Bolsheviki rather than against Russia.

Another communication is addressed to the soldiers and says that the crisis has come. It assures those that are wounded that they will receive aid from the government and gives further assurance that the govenment will care for dependents of those killed in battle.

Owing to the critical conditions, volunteers are coming in on every side, school teachers, students, boy scouts, civil servants and ministerial clerks who were previously exempted. The enlistment of students has been so great that Warsaw University is closed.

Hundreds of girls and women are joining the service. Yesterday a battalion of women with women officers paraded through the streets. It was the first time women guards with women officers had paraded and they aroused great enthusiasm. Most of them were young girls with short shirt waists and their hair braided down their backs. Mixed with them were women 25 to 30 swinging market baskets, vanity boxes and parasols with hands that will soon be carrying arms.

Undoubtedly the Polish leader had come to realize that the war in which he was involved was not merely an extension of the traditional nationalistic animosities between the two countries. If that were not his true belief, however, he was at least astute enough to recognize that a crusade against Bolshevism had greater world propaganda value than a localized war for the preservation or extension of borders.

In addition, the support of Poland's Catholic population was more readily enlisted by the anti-communism theme.

At Lwów, Kościuszko Squadron mechanics uncrated new Balillas and assembled them for a series of test flights, with Lieutenant Rorison getting the unenviable opportunity to give each plane its baptismal hop. Major Fauntleroy and Captain Cooper, meanwhile, had gone to Warsaw to check on a variety of supply details and to discuss the recruitment of additional American flyers. In the latter regard, they sent a cable to Col. Benjamin F. Castle, a former West Pointer and pilot who had become acquainted with members of the squadron when he visited Poland as a civilian after World War I on business for a New York bank. The message, over Fauntleroy's signature, said:

> We need twelve enthusiastic pilots, good flyers, gentlemen; essential must pay expenses to Poland, accept Polish pay of 2,000 marks. Scout pilots preferable. Can offer only lieutenant's rank. Could American Flying Club help?

There was little else they could do after that except to wait for possible results from their appeal to the American financier. In the meantime, while the two officers were at Mokotów field, they were notified that Fauntleroy had been promoted to lieutenant colonel and would be placed in charge of the Third Aviation Group **Dyon** serving the Polish Sixth Army. Cooper, in turn, was officially designated commander of the Kościuszko Squadron. Newspaper correspondents in the capital city helped them celebrate their change of status with a party which broke up at six the following morning. One year earlier the two officers had just begun developing plans in Paris for their adventure against the Bolsheviks; and that was an anniversary milestone also worthy of an extra toast or two.

During the months which followed the unit's creation, the American volunteers and the Poles who flew with them

When the chips were down, the three Polish pilots who remained with the squadron from the arrival of the Americans to their demobilization served with distinction despite limited training and a few lapses due largely to patriotic zeal and youthful exuberance. Lieutenants Aleksander Seńkowski (above left), Władysław Konopka (above right) and Jerzy Weber (left) were appropriately decorated along with their comrades from the United States.

had been unusually fortunate in escaping Bolo counter fire. Only Lieutenant Noble had been wounded sufficiently to force his retirement. Lieutenant Graves had been killed, of course, but prior to enemy action; and Lieutenant Clark, who had given the Reds plenty of opportunity to shoot him out of the sky, had been sidelined instead by illness in Kiev. The original six-month contracts signed by the pilots had expired before the Polish spring offensive, so the continued presence of the men emphasized their dedication to the cause. During the Lwów interim, however, Ken Shrewsbury — the squadron's legal eagle — found it necessary to return to the United States; and to replace him, Captain Kelly rejoined the organization after several months of flight training. Consequently, when Captain Cooper received orders on July 12 to move the unit to Hołoby, approximately 90 miles to the northeast, his duty roster included (besides Kelly and himself) Corsi, Chess, Crawford and Rorison, plus the indefatigable Poles — Weber, Konopka and Seńkowski. The new commander was confidently pleased to leave Lwów with such veteran, combat-tested airmen, and yet he also was seriously concerned about being short-handed as combat flights resumed. He could hardly afford to lose any of them!

———

As the squadron train steamed out of Lwów for Hołoby on Tuesday, July 13, the pilots themselves took off at intervals from Lewandówka field to fly individual reconnaissance missions over various segments of the ill-defined front enroute to their new base. They reported troop activity around Brody, Łuck and Dubno, but the greatest concentration of men seemed to be along the Horyń River which meandered northward from the vicinity of Równe through Klewań to the Pripet marsh country. Polish units there had stiffened against Budenny's thrusts as they took advantage of trenches, barbed wire entanglements and gun positions left over from earlier Russo-German fighting. There was no evidence of cavalry being massed for a major attack as in the north, but the Bolsheviks were applying pressure with forces of varying strength all the way from the Dniester to the slough-lands beyond the Warsaw-Kiev railroad.

Captain Cooper himself flew out over the Brody area, generally east of Lwów. Conscientious, capable and obsessively self-reliant, he disappeared into the sky over the Styr River looking for Bolsheviks. He was partially successful — but the Reds were more so. As a consequence, the new commander of the Kościuszko Squadron did not arrive at Hołoby that night; as a matter of fact, many months were to pass before the details of his fate were to filter out of the Russian abyss. Cooper had worried about a shortage of pilots, but — confident as he was — he probably didn't even consider the possibilty that he might be the first to go.

It was not particularly unusual for a flyer to be marooned overnight somewhere or other, out of gas or grounded by a cantankerous engine, but Cooper's flight direction into the center of Budenny's dispersed forces was a disturbing factor. When no messages arrived from him during the night and when he failed to appear the following morning, the anxiety concerning his whereabouts began to grow. Some superstitious member of the group added to the general state of uneasiness by pointing out that Hołoby was the 13th field from which the unit had operated and that the captain (whose name — Merian C. Cooper — contained 13 letters) was lost on the 13th of the month.

Fortunately, Major Fauntleroy was at the new base, too, so he temporarily reassumed command of the squadron and added his own name to the flight list. While Cooper's absence was of considerable concern to his flying comrades, there was little time to bemoan his unknown misfortune. The Polish ground forces were in desperate need of information about the enemy's location and movement, so there could be no letup in reconnaissance activities. Also assigned to the Third **Dyon** at Hołoby was the 21st Bomber Squadron, formed earlier by Lieutenant Rayski after he had left the Kościuszko

Crawford Collection

Capt. Arthur H. Kelly, the only non-pilot among the American contingent of air-men, took flight training in Poland, but when he returned to his unit during the critical days of July, 1920, he flew as an observer in a two-seater from the 21st Bomber Squadron which shared the Hołoby field. On July 15 the plane to which he was assigned was shot down, and the tall, slender Virginian became the second Kościuszko member to lose his life.

At Hołoby the officers' mess was located under an open-air canopy (above). Enlisted personnel often ate alongside the squadron train in typical military style, especially when movement was imminent (below).

ranks. Most of the 21st's planes were old German A.E.G. C-IV two-seaters, and because of Captain Kelly's World War I experiences, he was adjudged the best qualified observer available for special scouting missions. Accordingly, he was sent out with Polish pilots on July 13 and 14, spotting Bolshevik patrols, new field gun emplacements and at least one cavalry concentration at rest in a small village. On the 15th he was again dispatched over the fluid front lines in the vital, continuing effort to determine Budenny's basic strategy.

It was generally expected that the Russian push would be northwesterly in the direction of Warsaw, but the possibility of a major drive on Lwów could not be overlooked. Consequently, the keen eyes of Captain Kelly were counted upon to note any giveaway signs of the enemy's ultimate intentions. Sadly enough, the jovial Irishman's string of luck had run out, and the A.E.G. did not return to Hołoby that night! (Weeks later the news arrived that Kelly and his pilot had both been killed when their bomber crashed into a ravine in Red-occupied territory. Peasants in the neighborhood had buried the two men in shallow graves near the wreckage, but the exact details of their fatal flight were never completely learned.)

The Hołoby jinx almost claimed another victim on the following day when Fauntleroy attacked a Bolo cavalry detachment. As he was concentrating on strafing the enemy column, heavy ground fire from a forested area nearby took him by surprise. A bullet ripped through his Balilla's main gas tank, and almost simultaneously he felt a searing pain in his right leg. His biggest concern, of course, was to keep his plane in the air as the escaping gasoline blew back into his face and seriously impaired his vision. The Balilla's engine choked and died from lack of fuel, and the careening ship dropped down in the direction of the Bolo horsemen galloping overland in eager anticipation of a crash. Once again the availability of the **nourrice** — the small emergency gas tank on the upper wing of the Italian plane — saved the life of an American pilot. Despite his problems, Fauntleroy managed to open the gravity-feed pipeline, and as he angled downward to treetop height, the engine caught hold just in time to avert disaster. Somehow the ex-A.E.F. test pilot called upon all the skills of his World War I experience as he guided the crippled machine in the direction of the Polish lines. Angry, saber-swinging riders screamed Cossack invectives as the potential prize escaped their grasp. Although Fauntleroy was still worried about fire in his petrol-soaked cockpit, he felt considerably more comfortable as he passed over trenches manned by friendly forces on the eastern edge of Łuck. He landed a few moments later and learned to his relief that his leg wound was not crippling. The next day anxious squadron members welcomed him back to Hołoby, and a detail of mechanics left immediately by truck to rescue the plane.

On July 18 Buck Crawford participated in a variation of the same script when he and Ed Corsi took off at 7 p.m. on a late-evening attack mission in the direction of the Horyń River. Before they left, they had exchanged farewells with Harmon Rorison, the jaunty little Tarheel who had never completely recovered from the effects of the broken ribs sustained when he crashed in a Ukrainian swamp two months earlier. Rorison's departure for the United States further eroded the squadron's dwindling supply of pilots, and as the lieutenant and captain cruised over enemy territory looking for potential targets, the prospects of an additional loss quickly developed. Before the Americans could launch an assault, the Bolsheviks opened fire from hidden emplacements on the ground, and (exactly as Fauntleroy had experienced) a stray bullet punctured the main gas tank of Crawford's Balilla. When his engine stalled, Buck hurriedly switched on his **nourrice**—but unlike Fauntleroy, he got no response from the emergency supply, and somehow he managed to control the heavy-nosed plane to a dead-stick landing on a rough but open field. Corsi, meanwhile, had witnessed his partner's impromptu descent, and as he circled overhead to determine the best course of action, he spied a detachment of Cossack cavalry (he recorded 15 in the logbook) charging crosscountry toward the grounded plane. Crawford apparently had seen the enemy horsemen too, because he abandoned his crippled Balilla on the run and scurried for the nearest patch of woods.

With machineguns blazing in a diving attack, Corsi tried to divert and scatter the Bolsheviks to give Buck time to find shelter. Unfortunately, the delaying action had only minimal effect, and as Crawford calculated the distance to the trees, he could tell that his odds for survival were growing slimmer by the moment. Then, just as he was about to give up hope, he glanced back at his plane and noticed that the engine had fired up again. The **nourrice** supply had worked after all. Evidently a water bubble or a bit of foreign matter clogging the gas line had been jarred loose in the landing, and by some mechanical miracle the motor had roared back into action. The big lieutenant didn't stop to figure out how it happened; instead, he reversed his field and dashed back to the slowly

The squadron trucks, crude and cumbersome as they were, proved invaluable to the unit, not only for supply purposes, but in the vital work of recovering downed planes.

moving aircraft with all the speed an ex-Lehigh fullback could muster.

He won the race, happily enough, and as he scrambled into the cockpit, the Cossacks bore down upon him like an angry nightmare out of the tales of Genghis Khan. The Balilla responded to Crawford's heavy throttling, but as it bounced across the rutted ground, it hit an obstacle of some sort (possibly an irrigation ditch) which seriously damaged a wheel and cracked one of the longerons in the fuselage. For an instant, it seemed that the plane would crumble into a tangled heap just yards away from the pursuing Bolos; then, almost miraculously, the tiny ship righted itself and took to the air. According to another version of the legendary escape, the errant Balilla mowed part of a wheat field with its propeller and carried off a section of split rail fence on its landing gear as it eluded the saber slashes of the thwarted Reds. Dusk was settling in as Corsi wig-wagged a parting salute with his plane before returning to Hołoby. Crawford, with not enough gas to reach the squadron field, pancaked down at Łuck where he found auto transportation for the 50-mile trip to the Kościuszko train. He arrived at 3 a.m., and again the mechanics were dispatched by truck to retrieve another botched up Balilla.

––––––

At Hołoby the Kościuszko Squadron operated entirely from its mobile railroad base. The return to combat had not been particularly gratifying, especially with the still unexplained absence of Cooper and Kelly haunting the remaining pilots. To make matters worse, several cases of typhus fever were diagnosed among the enlisted personnel. It was difficult to maintain exuberance in the course of extended retreat without any additional aggravations. On the southern front the forces of General Budenny continued to press forward against begrudging Polish resistance, but the direct engagements of troops were generally scattered and indecisive. That, too, had an effect on morale as there was no specific rallying point to generate elan. From the air it was impossible to determine the Bolsheviks' primary plan of action: whether the main campaign would be aimed at Warsaw or if Lwów and then Kraków would be the principal objectives.

Rumors of peace proposals further confused the issue as the combined armies of General Tukhachevsky advanced toward the Polish capital in the north. On the international scene, it suddenly (but belatedly) became obvious to the Allied Powers that the Reds had more in mind than border alignments. An Associated Press dispatch from Paris on July 22 announced:

> The Allies have decided to take measures to give prompt military aid to Poland if necessary, it was learned today.
> A French commission led by Jules J. Jusserand, French ambassador to the United States home on leave, and including Gen. [Maxime] Weygand, right hand man of General Foch . . . . left today for Warsaw to promise succor to the Poles. On the same train was a British commission consisting of Lord D'Abernon, British minister to Berlin, General [Percy] Radcliffe and Sir Maurice Hankey. They were authorized to generally assure the Poles of aid and supplies if the Bolsheviks actually invaded Poland.
> It is stated unofficially that this means troops if they are required.

On the same day, an AP story from Washington, D.C., reported:

> Army officers and officials of the State Department generally were frankly pessimistic as to the ability of France and Great Britain to place armies in Poland in time to check the Russian advance before Warsaw falls, and many of them were skeptical of the power to drive their

war-weary people into the struggle without a
serious unbalancing of domestic affairs . . . .
For the present it was indicated at the State
Department the part of the United States will
be that of an interested observer. Steps already
have been taken to remove from the area such
Americans as may wish to leave.

The remaining members of the Kościuszko Squadron
were considerably more than mere "interested observers."
They were honoring a personal commitment which they considered valid and worthwhile, so they were understandably
disappointed by the lethargic response to Polish appeals at
home. Directly related to their situation was the fact that in
New York City Colonel Castle had succeeded in recruiting almost two dozen flyers who were willing to join the unit at
Hołoby, but governmental red tape had frustrated his efforts. In desperation he finally sent the following telegram
to President Wilson:

During the past three months at least half of
American aviators in Kościuszko Squadron
which has been fighting against Bolsheviki in
Poland have been killed, wounded or reported
missing. On July second I received cable from
Major Cedric Fauntleroy, then commanding the
squadron, requesting my assistance in securing
replacement pilots for his squadron. Since that
time twenty three brave American aviators
volunteered to go to Poland at their own expense
in order to fight for the continued existence of
the country whose independence was evoked
largely through your splendid appeal to the
world in nineteen eighteen. The volunteers ask
nothing from our government except permission
to leave the country and sail for Danzig at
earliest possible date. I am informed by those
who already have requested passports that State
Department will not issue same to Americans

who desire to go to Poland. May I not ask you to cause State Department to make special exception in the case of these splendid young Americans who are only emulating the fine example of their comrades who have already fought for Poland and those other valiant Americans who composed the Lafayette Escadrille during the great war.

Under the circumstances it was doubtful whether the Kościuszko Squadron would ever receive any replacement pilots in time to do much good. In the meantime, throughout the entire young Polish Air Force, conditions of supply and personnel had degenerated to a point of virtual hopelessness. Historian Jerzy B. Cynk, in recounting the gloomy period, wrote: ". . . . the equipment crisis worsened week by week. Frequent changes of airfields and landings on emergency sites during the rapid retreat resulted in an even higher attrition rate, and as the aeroplanes could not be repaired or evacuated in time, several squadrons lost their entire flying equipment. In July the situation became catastrophic; on the 25th of that month . . . . all the twenty squadrons put together had only thirty-one airworthy machines at their disposal."

———

When word reached Hołoby that the Bolsheviks had captured Dubno southeast of Łuck and that pressure was being maintained all along the sprawling front, a decision was made to move the Kościuszko Squadron farther westward beyond the Bug River to the village of Uściług, almost straight north of Lwów. The transfer was made on July 24, and the new location had an almost immediate effect on morale because of the improved living conditions. The typhus threat was continual, so the opportunity to abandon the boxcars for cleaner quarters was obviously welcomed. In a letter to Ken Shrewsbury, Buck Crawford disclosed that Uściług offered "a good swimming hole and a splendid chateau to live in." (For diversion during the warm summer evenings when they weren't flying, the pilots shot fish in the river, and suitless swimmers retrieved the finny victims for the squadron cook.) Meanwhile, the Third **Dyon** claimed most of Fauntleroy's time, so—for all practical purposes—only Crawford, Corsi and Chess of the original American volunteers remained on duty with the ever-decreasing unit.

Chapter XII

Tenacity at Lwów; Triumph at Warsaw

As the month of July, 1920, passed into history, the fate of Poland seemed quite predictable to world observers. The Polish spring offensive against an unprepared enemy had resulted in shortlived triumphs for Marshal Piłsudski, the analysts admitted; on the other hand, the Bolsheviks' retaliatory campaign was a well conceived maneuver which would crush the Polish dream and bring about a new alignment of power in Europe. The fact that Tukhachevsky ignored both French and British warnings by crossings into the traditional territory of Poland was clear indication that a decision had been made to carry the battle to Warsaw and beyond. With the Reds only hours away from the capital city on the Vistula, the discussion of help from afar seemed highly academic.

In Berlin Gen. Erich Ludendorff, the bellicose German war leader, offered to raise an army of a million and a half men to fight the Bolsheviks in exchange for the return of Posen (his birthplace) and the withdrawal of certain provisions of the Versailles Treaty. In a memorandum on the "dangers of Bolshevism" released on July 28, Ludendorff warned:

> Poland's fall will entail the fall of Germany and Czechoslovakia. Their neighbors to the

north and south will follow . . . . Let no one believe it will come to a stand without enveloping
Italy, France and England. Not even the seven
seas can stop it . . . . Then it will be too late and
civilization will crumble. And the cause will be
the abtuseness of government and lethargy of
the bourgeoise, as the latter likes to stay quietly
at home on days of decisive events.

The time of crisis had come, and despite belated offers
of help, Poland would have to face the fateful hour relatively
alone. Only a limited number of foreign volunteers already
on the scene—like the American members of the Kościuszko
Squadron—and the residual Ukrainian force from the agreement with Petlura would be of any value to Polish armies preparing themselves for the final confrontation. General Rozwadowski, who had participated in the realization of Merian
Cooper's unique proposition, returned to Warsaw from his
liaison post in Paris to become chief of the general staff.
Conscripts and volunteers swelled the ranks of the defending
forces; even the socialists and labor organizations responded
with the formation of several loyal workers' battalions when
it became clearly evident that the future of the homeland was
mortally threatened. It was also time for prayer, and Father
Pacificus Kennedy, O.F.M., in an article entitled "Help of the
Half-Defeated" recalled the fervent appeals:

In every Catholic church in Poland a novena
was begun on August 6, by order of the hierarchy, in preparation for the Assumption. That
same night Piłsudski locked himself in his study
in the Belvedere Palace. Through years of exile,
imprisonment a n d h o p e he had worn upon
his breast a **ryngraf** [shield] of Our Lady, and
through the dark hours of the night he prayed
to her. By dawn of the second day of the novena,
he had devised a plan for the defense of Warsaw.

Charles J. Phillips, an official of the Red Cross,

says that after the Masses on Sunday, August 8, one hundred thousand Varsovians marched in procession from one church to another—with the Bolsheviks only 25 miles away! Since all able-bodied men were fighting at the front or digging trenches in Warsaw, only women, children, old men and wounded warriors were in this line of march. "But with that procession—7 hours long —of praying, singing people, something had to come to drown the Soviet thunders," says Phillips, "a sound so vigorous and full-voiced that it seemed more like a supplication. It was a cry of defiance to the approaching enemy."

Whether by divine inspiration, on the advice of General Weygand or in consultation with his own officers, Marshal Piłsudski did create a master strategy to govern all Polish forces in the last-ditch effort to stem the Bolshevik invasion. Order No. 8358/3, published by the Supreme Command and signed by General Rozwadowski, was issued in the evening of August 6, and the massive realignment of troops to achieve the plan's objectives began immediately.

Instead of the existing two major fronts, three combat zones were designated. Gen. Józef Haller was put in command of the Northern Front which extended from Pułtusk directly north of Warsaw to Dęblin near the confluence of the Vistula and Wieprz Rivers 60 miles southeast of the capital. Piłsudski himself took personal responsibility for the Central Front which stretched from Dęblin generally along the Bug River to Brody on the Lwów-Równe rail line. The Southern Front, commanded by Gen. Wacław Iwaszkiewicz, completed the arc from Brody to the Dniester River. From these broad defensive positions, Marshal Piłsudski proposed to play his trump card. Tukhachevsky had ordered that Warsaw should be occupied "by August 12 at the latest," and based on that Bolshevik deadline, the Poles had less than a week to prepare for the final showdown.

Speaks Collection

Buck Crawford (right) became the third and final American commander of the Kościuszko Squadron at Kroczów. His predecessors were co-founders Cedric Fauntleroy (left) and Merian Cooper (center). Though he was born in Pennsylvania, Crawford listed his residence as Wilmington, Delaware. Like Cooper, he had been a prisoner of the Germans during World War I.

While the eyes of the world were focused on the dramatic activities centered around the Polish capital, the Kościuszko Squadron—despite its reduced flying force—was ready for any assignment the high command might have for it. At Usciług a limited number of flights was recorded, and most of these were for reconnaissance and communications purposes. On August 3 another pilot went on the inactive list temporarily when Lieutenant Weber piled up his Albatros on the squadron field during a somewhat unexplainable high-speed landing. For the second time in less than three months, he suffered painful head and shoulder injuries; and when he was sent off to the aid station for treatment, the unit's flying strength dropped to five.

On the same day Weber was hurt, the train was packed again and re-located at Korczów, half way on a line between Lwów and Usciług. Buck Crawford, whose captaincy was forthcoming, officially took command of the squadron at that time, because Fauntleroy was busy elsewhere and it appeared quite obvious that Cooper was never coming back. An Associated Press story, datelined Warsaw, August 5, included the following:

> The American aviators with the Kościuszko Squadron have been battling with General Budenny's cavalry and infantry at Sareth, where the Soviets are making no headway. Parts of the squadron were engaged yesterday at Mikileczl where they met Cossacks and a body of infantry. The losses to the enemy were heavy here, with 1,600 killed and a large number wounded.

On the sixth day of August, while Marshal Piłsudski was preparing to unveil his plan of deployment, all planes were grounded by a saturating rain. For three days the men sat in the boxcars, waiting for the weather to change and wondering what was in store for them in the hours and days ahead. The war was going badly for Poland, they knew, and right then—when the situation was the bleakest—there was very little they could do to help. What they didn't know, of course, was that the gigantic and complex shifting of land forces called for in Piłsudski's strategy was already underway and that they would soon be committed to a specific final action of historic dimensions.

The weather cleared sufficiently on August 8 for Crawford to fly to the west in search of alternate fields in case of another breakthrough. Corsi did the same thing on the ninth until he was forced to return to Korczów because of a blinding fog. On the tenth Lieutenant Weber flew back to the unit from Lwów, and Captain Konopka was sent out on a dispatch-dropping mission. When he returned from the routine flight just before noon and approached for his landing, it was quickly obvious to the ground crew that he was having trouble. Either his Albatros was acting up or he himself couldn't judge distances on the small field. As he made his first pass heading directly for the hangar and train, he overshot his mark, decided not to touch down and then roared up over the boxcars with only a few feet of clearance. He circled widely for another try, and again he miscalculated the runway. Twice the Albatros bounced high, and after the wheels hit the ground the third time, Konopka apparently realized he could never stop without a smashup, so he gave the plane full throttle, hoping to rise above the telegraph wires and the parked train.

Unfortunately, he couldn't get the Albatros to climb fast enough, and while flying at top speed, he plowed straight into the open door of the officers' kitchen car. It all happened so quickly that everyone who saw the freakish exhibition stood open-mouthed as the plane's wings were sheared off by the door frame while the motor disappeared inside, slamming into the opposite door which was closed. There was a fire in the stove in the car because the cook was preparing the noon meal, but luckily the plane did not burn. The pilot was pulled from the wreckage immediately, still alive but bleeding profusely from a severe laceration alongside his left eye, probably caused by his smashed goggles. After first-aid treatment revealed no apparent broken bones, he was rushed off to the nearest hospital. (The logbook doesn't record it, but according to squadron lore, the cook—who providentially wasn't standing in the doorway—was bounced against the car's ceiling and came down in a sitting position atop the hot stove. Supposedly he was found some time later perched in a water trough cooling his bottomside.)

Whether or not Konopka would ever return to the squadron was questionable. Weber's recovery maintained the flying roster at five, however, and after the momentary shock of the kitchen calamity, operations quickly reverted to normal. On August 11 Corsi and Chess flew over enemy lines to the east of Korczów and attacked Bolshevik cavalry near the Styr River. Later in the morning Crawford scouted the same general area and reported "plenty of Bolos." That afternoon the Kościuszko Squadron was transferred back to its birthplace at Lwów in an ironic turn of events. As the battle for Poland reached its most crucial juncture, the American volunteers (three of them, plus Colonel Fauntleroy at **Dyon** headquarters) were back in the historic city where Merian Cooper had witnessed an earlier siege which motivated him to cast his lot as a fighting man with Marshal Piłsudski in the first place.

———

The role of the Kościuszko Squadron in the climactic phase of the Polish-Russian War was quite simply defined: to support the forces of General Iwaszkiewicz on the Southern Front in any way possible, to defend the city of Lwów and to keep General Budenny so busy that he could not divert his troops to the battle for Warsaw.

The latter factor was most critical to the Polish cause. If Budenny could not be detained in Galicia, he would be free to combine with Tukhachevsky in a pincers movement on the capital. Moreover, he would be in a position to attack the rear

(Above and Opposite Page).
Lieutenant Konopka was a lucky survivor of a freakish accident at Korczów when he apparently misjudged distances on a landing approach and crashed his plane into the open door of the officers' kitchen car. Fortunately no one was standing in the doorway where the motor came to rest (above), and despite the tangle of shattered wings and plywood fuselage (above and below, opposite page), the pilot was not killed.

of a special strike force under General Śmigły-Rydz near Dęblin with which Piłsudski proposed to ambush the Russian commander-in-chief once the latter had committed his troops to an assault on Warsaw. There was little question but that the Cossack leader possessed in his divisions the balance of power to assure a Bolshevik triùmph on the Vistula. Keeping him out of the fight, then, was a major element of the Polish strategy.

As soon as the squadron was re-situated in the familiar accommodations at Lewandówka field, flying activity picked up almost immediately. If Budenny planned to attack Lwów before he turned his attention northward, the Kościuszko pilots proposed to convince him of their presence before the fight was over. Prior to the anticipated assault, however, it was decided to move most of the unit's mobile transport to Przemyśl just in case sudden evacuation became necessary; only ten cars were kept at the airdrome.

As it turned out, Budenny—whether by his own choice or someone else's—did choose to besiege Lwów, and flying primarily in support of the Polish Sixth Army, the Kościuszko Squadron was injected into the heart of the battle. Beginning on August 15, dawn-to-dusk flights were scheduled against the on-coming enemy. Because of the shortage of pilots, Colonel Fauntleroy flew combat missions whenever he could. The airmen bombed and strafed cavalry columns, infantry detachments, wagon trains and railroad cars. On the 16th, for instance, the logbook recorded 18 sorties, even though Buck Crawford was grounded by illness. Weber flew five separate missions, Chess and Seńkowski four each, Fauntleroy three and Corsi two. The same number of flights was tallied on the following day with Weber again completing five, Corsi and Seńkowski four, Chess three and Fauntleroy two. It was a gruelling pace which threatened to take its toll of men and machines—but the Bolsheviks were certainly made aware of the squadron's existence.

Fauntleroy and Crawford worked together closely when the latter assumed command of the squadron following Cooper's disappearance. Though he was busy with his new duties at Group headquarters, Fauntleroy continued to fly occasional missions in Kościuszko planes when pilot strength was seriously depleted.

To keep himself busy while his comrades were pummeling the **Konarmiya**, Crawford wrote a long letter to Ken Shrewsbury which traced the unit's moves after the latter's departure and which included a report of his own incapacitation in the following excerpt:

This Corona is now rated to be one of my most valuable possessions. I have dissected it, fed it with oil and new ribbons so that it works fine. I might add that the present owner is thot to be one of the swiftest and most efficient typists in all Poland . . . . From Korczów we moved to Lwów where Fauntleroy received the Fifth, Sixth and Fifteenth Squadrons. We have been here about a week. I have been flying a lot and crashing about on my Harley Davidson, amidst the derisive hoots of the general populace. About two days ago I contracted a rotten case of chills and fever . . . . However, I am now in the Hotel George, with nothing to do but order up various beers and wines in a vain effort to cool my fevered brow.

The Bolos are twenty kilometers away and coming like a whirlwind . . . . Everyone is working very hard now. Yesterday, with four pilots, the squadron made twenty-one flights [the logbook showed five flyers and 18 missions], and each pilot averaged more than six hours. Corsi dropped a bomb thru his tail, the same as you did in Berdichev . . . . The people here have great confidence in Gen. Iviscavitch [sic], our old friend from Tarnopol. By the way, I saw five Bolo planes on the ground just east of Tarnopol the other day. I was about one hundred and fifty meters high with bum guns. Two Fokkers took off after me but they had no chance with my Balilla . . . . My writing is becoming erratic, as from time to time I hear a tremendous rumbling below and I must jump up to see what is passing . . . . If we leave here, the next stop will be Przemyśl, then Kraków and from there it is only a short distance to the Hungarian border.

Crawford's letter indicated no defeatism, but it did reveal that the men were not overlooking a possible escape route.

As the Bolshevik pressure increased on Lwów, the squadron did make a precautionary move to Przemyśl on the 18th, but that was the extent of its westward withdrawal. On the 24th it was back at Lewandówka; the City of the Lion had not fallen; and Budenny never got away to help Tukhachevsky. Piłsudski's plan (with on-the-scene modifications and several fortuitous developments) had worked! His special force sliced off the over-eager Russians who had by-passed Warsaw on the north leaving their left flank vulnerably exposed; and as the battle progressed, Polish elements capitalized on the ensuing confusion to expand the counter offensive into a rout. For weeks the world's press had predicted an inevitable war-ending victory for the Bolsheviks on the Vistula—and then the situation took an unexpected one hundred and eighty degree turn. American newspapers—generally more interested in the Olympic Games at Antwerp and the final ratification of the Women's Suffrage amendment—reflected the historic military reversal in their headlines, like the ones below which appeared in a typical Midwestern small town daily, the Yankton (S. D.) **Press and Dakotan:**

August 16: Russian Troops Nearing Warsaw
August 17: Russians Lose Before Warsaw
August 19: Russian Forces Are Retreating
August 20: Polish Success Is Continuing
August 23: Russian Forces in Full Retreat
August 25: Soviet Meets Utter Defeat
August 26: Bolshevik Army Cut to Pieces

All of a sudden a Poland on the verge of desperation was a resurgent nation with new hope and a rekindled desire to drive the hated Bolsheviks back across the borders and into historical oblivion. At Lwów, news of the triumph at Warsaw had obvious morale implications, but it was not immediately possible to assess how important a role the Polish forces on the Southern Front—both land and air units—had played in the victory. Kościuszko Squadron members, for instance, could not have realized at the time that the Bolshevik high command was embroiled in an internal clash of personalities which directly affected the movements of Budenny's **Konarmiya.** History was to reveal later that messages from Tukhachevsky to the Cossack commander were delayed, garbled or disregarded until it became too late for Budenny to help even if he had hurried his troops to the Warsaw area.

Norman Davies, the British historian previously quoted, has advanced the thesis (supported by the writings of Leon Trotsky) that the **Konarmiya's** political officer, Joseph Stalin, was an indirect ally to the Polish cause. The future dictator's jealousy of I. T. Smilga, his counterpart with the Tukhachevsky forces, led him to order Budenny's siege of Lwów at precisely the time the **Konarmiya** should have been marching on Warsaw from the southeast. Later, when Budenny finally received and obeyed a directive on August 20 to withdraw from Lwów and turn northward, the Smilga-Tukhachevsky partnership had already failed in its mission. Trotsky made his charges pointedly: "If Stalin and Voroshilov and the illiterate Budenny had not had their own war in Galicia and the Red Cavalry had been at Lublin in time, the Red Army would not have suffered the disaster." (Credence was lent to the conjecture in the latter half of the 1930s when both Smigla and Tukhachevsky were shot during the Stalinist purges of that period.)

———

On August 24 Fauntleroy's appeal for additional pilots bore first fruit when Capt. T. V. McCallum arrived from London to join the squadron. Not much was known about the new man or his background when he arrived at Lewandówka. He gave his home address as Toronto, Canada, and attributed his flying skills to service in the British Royal Air Force. Unfortunately, no one was granted the time to know him better. Anxious to become part of the flying team, McCallum received permission on the final day of August to try his hand with a Balilla for the first time. He had been duly cautioned about

Capt. T. V. McCallum

Capt. T. V. McCallum, in his first flight as a squadron member on August 31, 1920, lost control of his Balilla and died instantly in the ensuing crash. Crewmen viewed the remains of the plane which burst into flames on impact.

AMERYKANOM POLEGŁYM
W OBRONIE POLSKI
W LATACH 1919-1920

TO AMERICAN HEROES
WHO GAVE THEIR LIVES
FOR POLAND 1919-1920

The final resting place of Captain Kelly, Captain McCallum and Lieutenant Graves in the Cemetery of the Defenders of Lwów (opposite page) was a shrine of honor when the Poles of the city were able to fulfill their pledge to provide perpetual care at the site. After Yalta the burial ground came under Communist control and all reference to the American heroes was obliterated (below).

The Institute of Marshall Jozef Pilsudski, New York, and The Historical Institute of General Wladyslaw Sikorski, London.

Fenn Collection

A flying eagle with wreath, the "wings" of a Polish pilot.

the trickiness of the short-winged, nose-heavy Italian planes, so when he took off without ceremony in the early afternoon, the event was considered strictly routine and inconsequential. The tiny ship climbed to a thousand feet without difficulty, after which the young officer circled the field once to familiarize himself with the controls. Then, to the dismay of squadron crewman watching the test flight from below, the Balilla banked sharply and fell off suddenly into a screaming nosedive. McCallum was unable to fight his way out of the full-throttle **vrille,** and the uncontrolled machine plummeted to the ground in the plaza of the Lwów railway station. A ball of flame engulfed the battered aircraft on impact, and the relatively unknown newcomer perished instantly.

Less than ten months earlier Lt. Edmund Graves had died under similar circumstances in the same city and had become a symbol of the Kościuszko Squadron's commitment to the war ahead. Captain McCallum's death, on the other hand, epitomized a task completed. The two men were buried beside one another in the Cemetery of the Defenders of Lwów. A few weeks later they were joined by Capt. Arthur H. Kelly, whose body was located and returned to the squadron for appropriate honors.

―――――

As their volunteered service in defense of another nation's freedom had taken the lives of Graves, Kelly and McCallum, the Kościuszko Squadron had, in turn, inflicted the wages of war on an unknown number of the enemy. Isaak Babel, a Russian writer who served with Budenny's forces in the Polish campaign, portrayed dramatically the impact of the American flyers on the men of the Konarmiya:

> Troop leader [Pavel] Trunov pointed out the four specks in the sky, four bombers sailing in and out of the swanlike clouds .... machines of the Air Squadron of Major Faunt-le-ro. Trunov started leveling his machinegun .... The planes

were flying into our station ever more closely, clumsily creaking up to their full height before diving down and looping the loop, a pink ray of sunlight on their wings . . . . The major and his bombers showed considerable skill. They dropped down to three hundred meters and shot up first Andrushka and then Trunov. None of the shots fired by our men did the Americans any harm . . . . So after half-an-hour, we were able to ride out and fetch the corpses. We carried the riddled body of Trunov to the town of Sokal. All his wounds were in his face, his cheeks punctured all over, his tongue ripped out. We washed him as best we could, placed a Caucasian saddle at the head of his coffin, and dug him an honourable grave next to the cathedral in the municipal gardens in the very centre of the town.

An Epilogue

Heroes of a Forgotten War

Miltary action in the Polish-Russian War was ended by terms of an armistice which went into effect at midnight on October 18, 1920. With the cessation of hostilities, the mission of the Kościuszko Squadron was completed, but the story of the redoubtable aviation unit did not conclude that abruptly.

After the battle of Warsaw and the siege of Lwów, squadron members continued to fly over the disintegrating front lines, mostly for reconnaissance purposes, as the actual fighting tapered away to spasmodic clashes of smaller patrols and outposts. General Budenny and the **Konarmiya** (with Joseph Stalin still in control) departed for the Crimea, licking their wounds along the way. After a final defeat at Zamość north of Lwów, they were exhausted, disheveled and decimated in numbers, but they were not in truth a vanquished force, as Gen. Nicholaievich Wrangel was to learn in the months which followed.

The members of the Kościuszko Squadron were tired, too, and their ranks had also been depleted—but their heads were held high and they were proud of what they had accomplished. A translated extract of an order from the Polish General Staff, dated September 1, 1920, indicated that Poland likewise was pleased with their contributions to the war effort:

The Squadrons Nos. 5, 6, 7 (Kościuszko) and
15 under the command of Chief of Aviation of

the 6th Army, Lt. Col. Pilot Faunt-le-Roy have during the 16th and 17th of August of this year accomplished 129 flights during which they dropped 7,700 klg. of bombs and used 16,700 machinegun bullets.

Figures show, most clearly, the resulting work done by the squadrons under Lt. Col. Pilot Faunt-le-Roy. The activities of the squadrons of the 6th Army in the battles with the Cavalry Army of Budenny were directed with the greatest efficiency. The extraordinary fighting of the squadrons is the fruit of the organizing ability and unlimited energy of Lt. Col. Pilot Faunt-le-Roy; thanks are due him for the idealistic and enthusiastic sacrifice for Poland's cause. Expressions of gratitude are also due to the commanders, flying and ground personnel of the 5th, 6th, 7th and 15th Squadrons without whose combined efforts these results could never have been accomplished. All of these men, having shown exceptional bravery in the last battles over Lwów, are to be recommended for distinction without delay.

> Chief of Staff
> /-/Rozwadowski
> Lieutenant-General

In time, all of the surviving Kościuszko pilots who served during the active fighting received Poland's highest award for valor, the **Virtuti Militari**. Even before the armistice papers were signed at the peace conference at Riga, capital city of Latvia, Gen. Stanisław Haller came to Lewandówka field on October 2 to confer the honor upon Crawford, Corsi, Konopka, Weber, Chess and Seńkowski. Noble had received his medal before he left the Red Cross hospital in France, and Shrewsbury and Rorison were decorated at a special ceremony in Washington, D.C., attended by Jan Paderewski and Gen. John J. Pershing.

As the war wound down, several news bulletins—possibly more fanciful than factual—emanated from Poland. One widely disseminated story reported:

> Warsaw—Polish army intelligence officers report that Moscow offered a reward of 1,000,000 rubles for the capture, dead or alive, of Major Cedric E. Fauntleroy .... commander of the Polish air forces of the Southern Front. General

The Kościuszko Squadron just prior to demobilization consisted of (left to right, on landing gear): Konopka and Murray; (on ground): Weber, Poznański, Orzechowski, Corsi, Crawford, Speaks, Chess, Evans, Maitland, Seńkowski and Garlick.

Speaks Collection

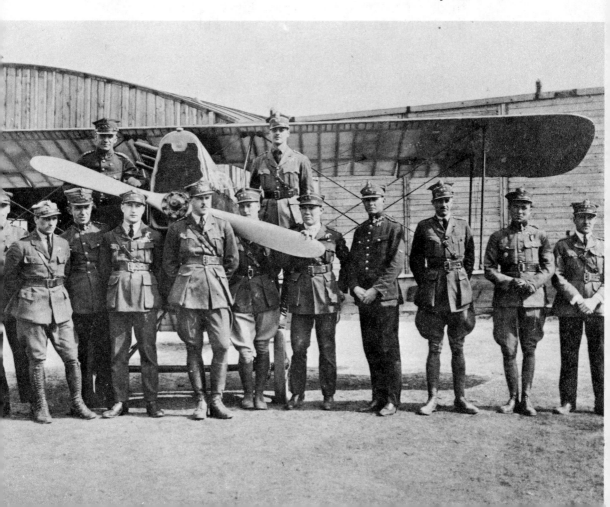

> Budenny's failure to take Lemberg [Lwów],
> when the Bolsheviks made the August drive upon
> Warsaw, is attributed by Lenin and Trotsky
> chiefly to the fight against the Cossacks from
> the air.

Although General Budenny's personal living accommodations were never mentioned in logbook reports, another article headlined "American Flyers True to National Creed" was popularly reproduced by newspapers in the United States:

> Warsaw—American flyers composing the Kościuszko Squadron of the Polish army have had
> many opportunities to bomb the train of six cars
> which General Budenny, the Bolshevik cavalry
> leader, used at the front, but they always refused
> to do so because they knew his wife and baby
> lived aboard the train. On several occasions
> when the Budenny Special was located by the
> Americans, they knew pretty well that the cavalry commander was at his traveling home
> for a visit with his wife and youngster, but they
> always let pass the chance to do him or his train
> harm.
> It was reported some time ago that Budenny
> had been wounded by a bomb dropped by one of
> the American flyers while he was engaged in one
> of his spectacular raids on the southern Polish
> front before the armistice was declared . . . .
> General Budenny is a Kuban Cossack and was
> a sergeant major in the old Imperial Russian
> army. He has been seen many times from the
> air by the Americans and is described as a short,
> stocky man with quite an intelligent countenance
> despite the wild outdoor life he has led for years.

———

Whether Colonel Castle's wire to the President did the trick or not, the U. S. State Department finally relented on its passport decision and permitted replacement officers for the

216

Kościuszko Squadron to depart for Poland. After governmental delay, they arrived in Lwów just before the armistice and too late for the shooting. Five of the new pilots remained with the unit until its final demobilization in the spring of 1921. Four of them—Thomas H. Garlick, John Inglis Maitland, Kenneth Malcolm Murray and John C. Speaks, Jr.—had joined the British Royal Air Force and were trained in Canada. Garlick, who had enlisted through the New York City recruiting office, received his commission and served in England, never reaching a front-line organization. Maitland, a native of Toronto, Canada, who had moved to Detroit with his parents as a youngster, made it to France where he was a member of the 54th and 80th Squadrons of the Royal Air Force. Speaks—son of a brigadier general who was later a U. S. Congressman from Columbus, Ohio—had one of the most active combat careers of any of the Kościuszko flyers. As a member of the RAF's 56th Squadron, he had been credited with the destruction of an enemy observation balloon and one German Fokker. (A second dogfight victory was never officially confirmed.) His aerial achievements had won him the British Distinguished Flying Cross. Murray, another New Yorker, had a special distinction, because he brought his own plane—a Sopwith Camel—with him. (In actuality, the privately-owned craft was purchased by the Polish government before it was shipped from the United States.) A fifth pilot—Earl F. Evans—was a cousin of Elliott Chess from El Paso. He had been graduated from ground school at the University of Texas, after which he enlisted in the U. S. Air Service and ultimately went to France as a member of the 49th Aero Squadron. An additional Polish officer—Capt. Antoni Poznański—was also assigned to the unit in its final months. Several other airmen checked in briefly with the Kościuszko command—including Charles E. Hays of Memphis, Tennessee, and S. T. Kauffman and Richard C. Allen, both of whom gave their next-of-kin addresses as Kansas City, Missouri—but their names appeared only a few times in the

An exception to the regular squadron fighter aircraft was this British Sopwith Camel, brought to Poland by Lt. Kenneth M. Murray.

logbook and then they were gone.

Although the late-comers did not experience direct combat with the Bolsheviks, they did fill an important role in the interim. The armistice of October 18 was just that—a temporary truce until a more permanent agreement could be reached. The Poles had won a tremendous victory at Warsaw, but while the Red Army was battered and beaten, it was not

Typical of American servicemen in any war, the Kościuszko Squadron pilots were partial to mascots. Spad, with Corsi and Crawford (above), was the first; Della, with Fauntleroy (above left and left) was with the unit until demobilization. According to the logbook, the flyers were also well acquainted with a pig named Theodora.

Corsi, Crawford and Shrewsbury Collections

The new pilots were as unfamiliar with the Albatros as the original American volunteers had been. However, they had the advantage of briefings based on experience from those who had flown the D.IIIs to Kiev and back again. Four of the "latecomers" to the squadron are, left to right, Thomas H. Garlick (standing on the wheel) John C. Speaks, Kenneth M. Murray and J. Inglis Maitland.

wiped out. There was always the possibility of renewed warfare during the winter or in the upcoming spring, and the Kościuszko Squadron remained ever ready to go back into action until the final peace treaty was signed at Riga on March 18, 1921.

Duty during the winter and early spring was not particularly demanding, and the young officers—for the most part—enjoyed their sojourn in Lwów. They played football and baseball during the appropriate seasons and installed a somewhat unprofessional golf course on Lewandówka field. They partied, too, and went on leave to Warsaw, Kraków and other points of interest. Reports in the logbook—so terse and serious during the war action—became less formal and were not always confined to the business of military aviation. The romantic trysts of Della, the squadron's canine mascot, were periodically recorded; and following immunization shots for typhoid, a waggish notation averred that "the squadron is now safe from coughs, colds, sore 'oles, easels, weasels, measles and pimples on the belly." The final entry on December 31 was the unmilitary-like pronouncement that "Lt. Weber was drunk for the last time in 1920."

———

The squadron had one item of unfinished business which wasn't resolved until shortly before the unit was officially disbanded. Captain Cooper's disappearance over enemy territory on July 13 of the previous year had remained a nagging mystery to his comrades, and though there was substantial evidence that he had been captured by the Bolsheviks, his ultimate fate had never been revealed. On April 26, 1921, a U. S. diplomatic representative in Latvia sent a cable to the Secretary of State which read:

> Merian Cooper, an American citizen formerly with Polish air service, who was imprisoned in Moscow under the name of Mosher, has just arrived Riga. He has reported for duty to the Poles by telegraph.

More than nine months had elapsed since the ill-fated flight to Hołoby. Thin but tough as bayonet steel, Cooper— according to one version of the story—had fled from Bolshevik prison guards near Moscow while on a railroad work detail. He and two Poles—a lieutenant and a corporal—took advantage of an inhumanly cold day to disappear from the

Durable and undaunted, Merian Cooper (center) escaped from a Russian prison near Moscow with the two Poles shown with him. Later he credited his survival to the tough training he had received at the U. S. Naval Academy.

labor detachment when the Red attendants became convinced that no one would attempt to flee under such brutal weather conditions. Traveling by night and hiding by day, the three men worked their way westward toward the Latvian border. On the few occasions when they were confronted by natives, Cooper played the role of a deaf mute, and the Polish officer—who spoke Russian—resorted to all the histrionic ability he could muster to protect their true identities. The dramatic escape was successful, of course, and the American pilot hurried to rejoin his squadron.

(Kenneth Murray, in a somewhat flowery article written for POLAND MAGAZINE in December of 1925, said that Cooper adopted the name of "Corporal J. Shane" and escaped from a wood-gathering crew with two Polish officers. These and other somewhat contradictory details of the American airman's imprisonment have had to be assembled piecemeal from his conversations, interviews, military records and personal correspondence. He always planned to write that part of the Kościuszko story himself before he died, but he waited too long and the opportunity was denied him.)

On July 13 Cooper's flight over the lines enroute to the new base at Hołoby took him to the vicinity of Równe. There he spotted a large patrol of enemy horsemen, and as he dropped down for a better view, a burst of machinegun fire smashed into the plane's motor. Cooper survived the ensuing crash and was dragged from the cockpit by the Bolo cavalrymen. He told friends later that he was saved from immediate execution when he showed the Cossacks his calloused hands (burned when the Germans shot him down in World War I) and insisted that he was a worker impressed into service and not a bourgeois officer.

He was wearing surplus A. E. F. underwear at the time, and when his captors stripped him of his uniform, he noticed a stenciled laundry mark and the name "Corporal Frank Mosher." From that moment he steadfastly maintained that he was a conscripted soldier and not an officer of the hated **Eskadra Kościuszkowska.** The ruse worked, and the life of the captain-turned-corporal was spared for the dubious alternative of incarceration in a Bolshevik prison.

The first word that Frank Mosher was really Merian Cooper reached Riga on October 1, 1920, and was immediately cabled to the U. S. State Department. On December 15 an Austrian officer, Leopold Politzer, who had recently been released from confinement in Russia, wrote a letter to the American Mission in Vienna which said:

> At the request of a member of the Mission's staff, with whom I spoke this morning, I give you the following information concerning the American gentleman in question:
>
> The gentleman's name is Merian C. Cooper. He is a Captain and his home is Jacksonville, Florida, U.S.A. Captain Cooper served in the Polish Army as organizer of military aviation during the Russian-Polish war, under the command of Major Cedric E. Fauntleroy. In the Spring of 1920 he was hurled to the ground in his burning machine, and fell into the hands of the Bolsheviks, who put him into prison at Moscow, where he is still kept under the most terrible conditions. Since Captain Cooper had a very bad name among the Bolsheviks and as his situation among them was a dangerous one, he gave a false name and searches for him must be made accordingly. The name is: Frank MOSHER, Corporal, No. 4608, at present Moscow, Alexandrowski-Lager (barracks).
>
> Captain Cooper very urgently asked me to lay stress on the fact that his real name be not mentioned on Russian territory, as this would only make the situation worse. I have to state again that Captain Cooper is living under most terrible conditions, is suffering from hunger, must do the lowest hard labor, is freezing and in continuous danger of being infected with illness. Captain Cooper is an American citizen and deserves quick help.

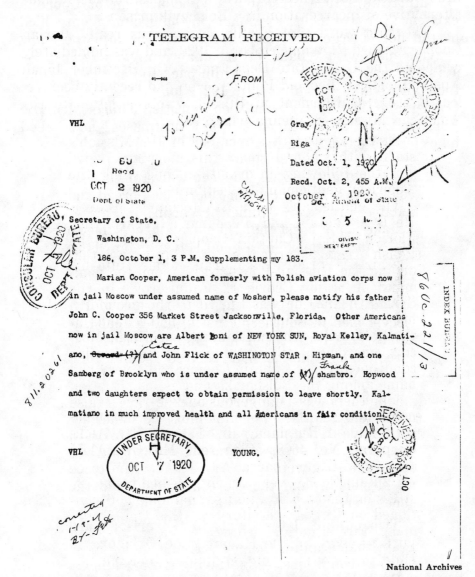

A generously stamped and initialed telegram from Riga to the U. S. State Department brought official news that Cooper was alive in a Moscow prison and that he was using an alias, "Corporal Frank Mosher."

Murray's article presented a vivid account of Cooper's existence for five months in a hole in the ground from which he did not emerge until he was thrown out into the snow "raving mad with typhus." Presumably he was rescued by a Tsarist physician who nursed him back to health, "stealing food and water for him." In 1927, long after his ordeal, Cooper himself wrote a small book entitled **Things Men Die For,** and in a chapter headed "Seven Christmases," he recalled his Yuletide experience in Russia:

> I love a good cigar. To sleep warm or to sleep cold, downy bed or cement floor, black bread and a dab of grease or a dinner at Voisin's in Paris— I make it my boast that they are all the same to me. But the smoke of a good Havana cigar is as the air of Paradise as I draw it deep into my lungs.
>
> And Orlanorf Petrovich, formerly one of the richest men in Southern Russia, had a real Havana. This little fat Armenian, who slept just three bunks from me, had received one in a food parcel. What a luxury in a Russian prison!
>
> I took stock of my scanty belongings. It did not take long. Here was something of tremendous value in Russia, a pair of shoes. They were two small for my swollen feet, but Orlanorf's feet were as a woman's. And I knew him to be an Armenian, and therefore a trader; and the shoes were worth more than the cigar.
>
> Two minutes later I was in the prison yard puffing away on the Havana, and Orlanorf, in childish joy, was trying on his new footgear.
>
> Our commandant, not a bad fellow, had permitted a Polish priest to come into the prison. In a damp stone cellar—once my prison cell— he was holding mass.

On the hard, cold stone floor were kneeling some hundred persons, attired in a strangely different assortment of nondescript garments, a few were well dressed, but most were in rags or near rags. The priest was hearing confession. He placed his hand over his eyes, in order not to see the person confessing. A woman knelt at his feet. She whispered the s t o r y of her sins in his ear. Beside her was the most famous woman blackmailer in Europe in her day, a marvelous musician who speaks a half dozen

Awaiting Cooper's return to Riga at the Warsaw train station were squadron members (left to right, in uniform): Crawford, Speaks, Fauntleroy and Maitland. Associated Press correspondent James P. Howe was between Crawford and Speaks, and Fauntleroy's wife—who accompanied the colonel back to Poland following a speech-making and recruiting trip to the U. S.—stood next to her husband.

Speaks Collection

The late-arrival pilots who kept the Kościuszko Squadron at fighting strength between the armistice and the treaty signing were decorated by the Polish government prior to their demobilization. Left to right were Lieutenants Evans, Maitland, Murray, Garlick and Speaks.

languages fluently. I looked curiously at the crowd. There was Count Szechenyi, the cousin of Gladys Vanderbilt's Hungarian husband; the little boy Crown Prince of Khiva, no Christian he, but looking on curiously at this infidel worship; a famous Russian scientist, dressed in padded cotton trousers and torn shirt; twenty different nationalities all mixed together, making as strange and heterogeneous a congregation as ever knelt together at the feet of a priest.

Out I went to look at the high walls of the prison, once a monastery and fort combined.

Col. Benjamin F. Castle (right), a New York banker and ex-military pilot, was the squadron's contact in the United States when new flyers were being recruited. Lieutenant Chess was among the greeters when the colonel visited the unit in Lwów shortly before demobilization.

For a moment I forgot where I was. I seemed to see clearly through the three-foot thickness of stone which kept me away from the world, the palmettos and orange groves on my own warm homeland. Then I remembered my strange prison mates at prayer on a dungeon floor.

"What a hell of a funny Christmas," I said aloud.

229

Following his escape from Bolshevik confinement, Merian Cooper (third from right) joined John Maitland and Colonel Fauntleroy in honoring their fallen comrades who were reinterred in the Cemetery of the Defenders of Lwów.

Cooper was reunited with his old Kościuszko Squadron comrades—and those who arrived in his long absence—on Sunday, May 8, in Warsaw. He was informed that he had been promoted to major shortly after his capture and that his new rank would be lieutenant colonel. Fauntleroy received the eagles of a full colonel and Buck Crawford became a major. To say the least, it was a joyous reunion!

On May 10 the squadron members reported to Belvedere Palace where Marshal Piłsudski—no longer skeptical of their capabilities—greeted the men warmly and decorated Cooper with the **Virtuti Militari** and the **K r z y ż W a l e c z n y c h**

(Cross of Valor) with two bars. The latter medal was also presented to Fauntleroy, with three bars; Crawford, three bars; Corsi, two bars; and Chess, one bar. From Belvedere the ceremonies moved to Mokotów field where General Haller awarded all of the squadron pilots the Haller medal. That night a festive dinner and dance were held at the officers' mess in honor of the American airmen.

Harmon Rorison (in uniform) and Kenneth Shrewsbury were decorated with the VIRTUTI MILITARI on March 14, 1921, at a special ceremony in Washington, D.C., attended by Jan Paderewski and Gen. John J. Pershing.

Shrewsbury Collection

(Above and opposite page).
The day before the American members of the Kościuszko Squadron were demobilized, Marshal Józef Piłsudski decorated Cooper, Fauntleroy, Crawford, Corsi and Chess with Poland's Cross of Valor. Cooper also received the VIRTUTI MILITARI, the nation's highest honor, which had been presented to the others earlier. The ceremony took place at Belvedere Palace, Warsaw.

The Kościuszko Squadron of the Polish-Russian War was officially demobilized the next day, May 11. A small land grant in Poland—which accompanied the **Virtuti Militari** decoration—was offered to the Americans, but they settled for a counter proposal. Their lesser holdings were combined into one larger unit which contained a comfortable chateau; and the resultant estate was turned over to the Polish Army for use as a convalescent home by the wounded soldiers of the free and independent nation of the White Eagle!

R O Z K A Z   P O C H W A L N Y
- . - . - . - . - . - . - . - . - . - . - . - . - . - . -
D L A
7 ESKADRY MYSLIWSKIEJ IM. KOSCIUSZKI.

W chwili, gdy Polska otoczona pierścieniem nieprzyjaciół w krawym wysiłku
zdobywa swą niepodległość, dziewięciu oficerów amerykańskich przybywa do Polski ażeby walczyć ramię przy ramieniu w myśl starej polskiej maksymy"za naszą
i waszą wolność".

Skromni obejściem, bohaterscy w walkach amerykańscy oficerowie wraz z
pułkownikiem FAUNT LE ROY na czele swem poświęceniem, dzielnością i odwagą
chcą rzucić rozgłos w świat cały, że Polska powstała i w krawych bitwach zdobywa swą niepodległość.

Natychmiast po przybyciu- do Polski pułkownik FAUNT LE ROY obejmuje 7-ą
Eskadrę Myśliwską, która otrzymuje nazwę im. Kościuszki, ażeby w myśl zasad
tego Męża i pod Jego imieniem dokonać tych czynów, do spełnienia których dążył nasz i jednocześnie wolnych Stanów Zjednoczonych bohater.

W pierwszych miesiącach pobytu w Polsce ginie we Lwowie śmiercią lotników
pilot Edmund GRAVES, który swemi śmiałemi lotami chciał uczcić dzień oswobo-
dzenia Lwowa, tak pamiętny dla każdego Polaka.

Nie wypocząwszy po walkach z ukraińcami, w których tak świetnie odzna-
czyli się swemi dzielnemi lotami amerykańscy oficerowie 7 Eskadry im.Kościuszki,
skoro tylko zabrzmiały pierwsze odgłosy silniejszych starć z bolszewikami,ofi-
cerowie ci dzięki olbrzymim wysiłkom organizują i ekwipują Eskadrę, wyruszając
natychmiast na front.

Nietylko nam lotnikom, lecz i całemu społeczeństwu polskiemu znane są
ze swej śmiałości i brawury ataki oficerów amerykańskich na dzikie hordy bol-
szewickie.

W walkach tych ginie bohaterską śmiercią kapitan- obserwator KELLY
Artur, a kapitan COOPER Merian, zestrzelony przez bolszewików, dostaje się
di niewoli, z której po okropnych moralnych i fizycznych cierpieniach ucieka,
przebywając piechotą przestrzeń z Moskwy do Rygi.

W próbnym locie ginie śmiercią lotników kapitan pilot MACCALUM.

Dziś, po zwycięsko zakończonej wojnie, po dokonaniu czynów, do których
dążył Kościuszko, młode Orły wolnej Ameryki odchodzą z naszego grona.

Za ten trud krwawy, za przetrwanie na posterunku w najcięższych chwilach
minionej wojny składam w imieniu Lotnictwa Polowego najgorętsze podziękowanie:

Pułkownikowi pilotowi	Cedric E. FAUNT LE ROY
Ppułkownikowi-pilotowi	Merian COOPER
Majorowi-pilotowi	George M. CRAWFORD
Kapitanowi-pilotowi	Edward CORSI
Kapitanowi-pilotowi	Carl CLARC
Kapitanowi-pilotowi	Harmen RORISON
Porucznikowi-pilotowi	Kenneth SHREWSBURY
Porucznikowi-pilotowi	Elliot CHESS
Porucznikowi-pilotowi	Kenneth MURRAY
Porucznikowi-pilotowi	Earl F.EVANS
Porucznikowi-pilotowi	Inglis MAITLAND
Porucznikowi-pilotowi	John SPEAKS
Porucznikowi-pilotowi	I.H. GARLICK.

A Tym, którzy swe życie poświęcili dla Polski - hołd wiecznej czci
i uznania.

Dzielnym i bohaterskim synom wolnej Ameryki Cześć.

SZEF LOTNICTWA POLOWEGO
/-/ St. JASIŃSKI
MAJOR-PILOT.

Warszawa dn. 10 maja 1921 r.

In addition to the decorations received by squadron members prior to their demobilization, they were cited in a commendation order issued on May 10, 1921, in Warsaw. A translation is printed on the opposite page.

Crawford Collection

TO MAJOR PILOT GEORGE CRAWFORD
KNIGHT OF "VIRTUTI MILITARI"
and "CROSS OF VALOR".

COMMENDATORY ORDER
to
No. 7 FIGHTER SQAUDRON — KOŚCIUSZKO

At the time when Poland was under enemy oppression during the struggle for independence, nine American officers arrived in Poland to fight arm to arm "FOR OUR AND YOUR FREEDOM."

They were very modest, but brave on the battlefield under the leadership of Colonel FAUNT LE ROY and wanted to tell the Free World that Poland won its own independence.

Immediately after they arrived in Poland Colonel FAUNT LE ROY became commanding Officer of No. 7 Fighter Squadron and changed the name to KOŚCIUSZKO to dedicate it to continued friendship between the United States and Poland.

During the first few months Pilot EDMUND GRAVES lost his life during a flight over Lwów, during which he wished to dedicate the Liberation of the CITY OF LWÓW.

Later the brave American Pilots of the Kościuszko Squadron continued to fight in the air against the bolsheviks in the first line of every battlefield.

Every Pole today knows about the heroism of the American Pilots during the war against the savage bolshevik hordes.

During these battles Captain-Observer ARTHUR KELLY was killed. Also Captain MERIAN COOPER was shot down by the bolsheviks and was imprisoned in terrible moral and physical conditions but managed to escape on foot from Moscow to Riga.

Captain Pilot McCALLUM was killed on a test flight.

Today, after a victorious conclusion of war over the enemy, the YOUNG EAGLES OF AMERICA are leaving us.

For their outstanding achievement and sacrifice and for enduring the war on behalf of the Polish Air Force may I offer the following Officers MY SINCERE THANKS:

Col. Cedric E. FAUNT LE ROY
Col. Merian COOPER
Maj. George M. CRAWFORD
Capt. Edward CORSI
Capt. Carl CLARK
Capt. Harmon RORISON
Lt. Kenneth SHREWSBURY
Lt. Elliot CHESS
Lt. Kenneth MURRAY
Lt. Earl F. EVANS
Lt. Inglis MAITLAND
Lt. John SPEAKS
Lt. I. H. GARLICK

Also for those who sacrificed their own lives for Poland we pay tribute and worship with appreciation—the COURAGEOUS AND HEROIC SONS OF FREE AMERICA WE SALUTE.

CHIEF OF STAFF OF POLISH AIR FORCE
St. JASINSKI
Major Pilot

WARSAW
May 10th, 1921

An Epilogue

The irony of this story, of course, is that the valorous achievements of the Kościuszko Squadron (like those of the A.E.F.) were transitory and then abruptly negated by the events of the decades which followed. World War II and its political aftermath saw another Soviet conspiracy accomplish what Tukhachevsky and Budenny were unable to do. Piłsudski's Poland—free for so short a time—was, in the eyes of many loyal exiled nationalists, again obliterated from the map of Europe.

In Lwów at the funeral of Lt. Edmund P. Graves on November 24, 1919, a speaker turned to the American pilots attending the services and said: "Tell your compatriots across the ocean that these noble remains will rest among friends; that we will encompass this grave with loving care; that each spring, flowers will bloom here and the memory of this fallen warrior will be linked with t h e names of our heroes." Appropriately, a colonnade was erected by the resting places of the three Kościuszko Squadron airmen—Graves, Kelly and MaCallum. Its inscription was a simple tribute in gratitude: "They died so that we can live free."

At 6 a.m. on the morning of August 25, 1971, tanks of the Communist regime rolled across the hallowed grounds at the Cemetery of the Defenders of Lwów. Graves, which had already been desecrated, and the monument to the Kościuszko flyers, which had already been defaced, were totally demolished by the massive treads of the war machines.

The promised flowers no longer bloomed.

Though Tadeusz Kościuszko died in Switzerland in 1817, his body was ultimately moved to Kraków where he was re-interred among Poland's kings and heroes. Wawel Hill in that city memorializes the Polish patriot.

Bibliography

The material for this book came chiefly from first-hand sources: the reminiscences, letters, memoirs and logbooks of the airmen who lived the unusual experience. The authors supplemented such primary data with background research into newspapers and other periodicals of the particular time frame, including **The Literary Digest, The Stars and Stripes, The New York Times** and various selected publications. Aircraft specifications were doublechecked in—

L'Aviazione Austro-Ungarica Sulla Fronte

Italiana 1915-1918 by Riccardo Cavigioli

Fighter Aircraft of the 1914-1918 War as compiled by W. M. Lamberton

The Albatros DI-DIII, No. 127 of Aircraft Profiles

Also Consulted Were:

Baedeker, Karl. **Russia: Handbook for Travellers,** New York: Charles Scribner's Sons, 1914.

Behlmer, Rudy. "Merian C. Cooper," **Films in Review,** January, 1966.

Chamberlain, W. H. **The Russian Revolution,** Vol. II. New York: The Macmillan Company, 1935.

Cooper, Merian C. **Things Men Die For.** New York: G. P. Putnam's Sons, 1927.

Corsi, Edward C. **Poland: Land of the White Eagle.** New York: Wyndham Press, 1933.

Cynk, Jerzy B. **History of the Polish Air Force, 1918-1968.** Reading, England: Osprey Publishing Ltd., 1972.

Davies, Norman. **White Eagle, Red Star.** London: Macdonald & Co., Ltd., 1972.

Dziewanowski, M. K. **Joseph Piłsudski: A European Federalist, 1918-1922.** Stanford, Calif.: Hoover Institution Press, 1969.

Eastern Provinces of Poland. London: The Polish Ministry of Preparatory Work Concerning the Peace Conference, 1944.

Halecki, Oskar. **A History of Poland.** New York: Roy Publishers, 1943.

Jackson, Robert. **At War with the Bolsheviks: 1917-20.** London: Tom Stacey, Ltd., 1972.

Bibliography

Kennedy, Pacificus, O.F.M. "Help of the Half-Defeated," **The Immaculate,** August, 1966.

Lwów and the Lwów Region. London: The Polish Ministry of Preparatory Work Concerning the Peace Conference, 1945.

Mitchell, David. **1919: Red Mirage.** New York: The Macmillan Company, 1970.

Mizwa, Stephen P. **Great Men and Women of Poland.** New York: The Macmillan Company, 1942.

Morrison, James F. **The Polish People's Republic.** Baltimore: The Johns Hopkins Press, 1968.

Murray, Kenneth Malcolm. **Wings Over Poland.** New York and London: D. Appleton and Company, 1932.

Romeyko, Marjan. **Ku-Czci Poległych Lotników.** Warsaw: Lucjana Zlołnickiego, 1933.

Smogorzewski, Casimir. **About the Curzon Line and Other Lines.** London: Free Europe Pamphlet No. 7, 1944.

Troscianko, Wiktor. "Profanation in Lwów," **East Europe Magazine,** May, 1972.

Voigt, F. A. **Poland, Russia and Great Britain.** National Committee of Americans of Polish Descent, Inc., undated booklet.

Wells, H. G. **The Outline of History,** Vol. II. Garden City, N. Y.: Garden City Books, 1949.

Illustration Index

A

B

E

F

G

H

L

Mc

M

Illustration Index

Murray, Kenneth Malcolm, Lt. — 215, 218, 220, 228, 234, 235

N

Noble, Edwin Lawrence, Lt. — 31, 32, 35, 63, 103, 121

O

Orzechowski, Zbigniew, Capt. — 63, 215

P

Packard truck — 158
Paderewski, Ignacy Jan — 27, 231
pani-wagons — 100
parachutes — 145
Pershing, John J., Gen. — 231
Piłsudski, Marshal Józef — 36, 153, 232, 233
Poland, map of — 124
Polish
   armoured train — 114
   cavalry units — 136
   infantry unit — 91
   medals — 121
   pilot wings — 117, 210
   tanks — 156
   women's battalions — 174, 175, 176

U

V

W

Index

A

Index

B

Index

Index

D

G

H

I

Mc

M

N

O

P

Index

R

Index

S

T

U

W

Index

Y

Z